IN A FLASH

CLINT WESTGARD

ALSO BY CLINT WESTGARD

Published by Lost Quarter Books
www.lostquarterbooks.com

This edition 2017

Cover image from
https://www.flickr.com/photos/geishaboy500/2326873674.

ISBN: 978-1-928035-15-2

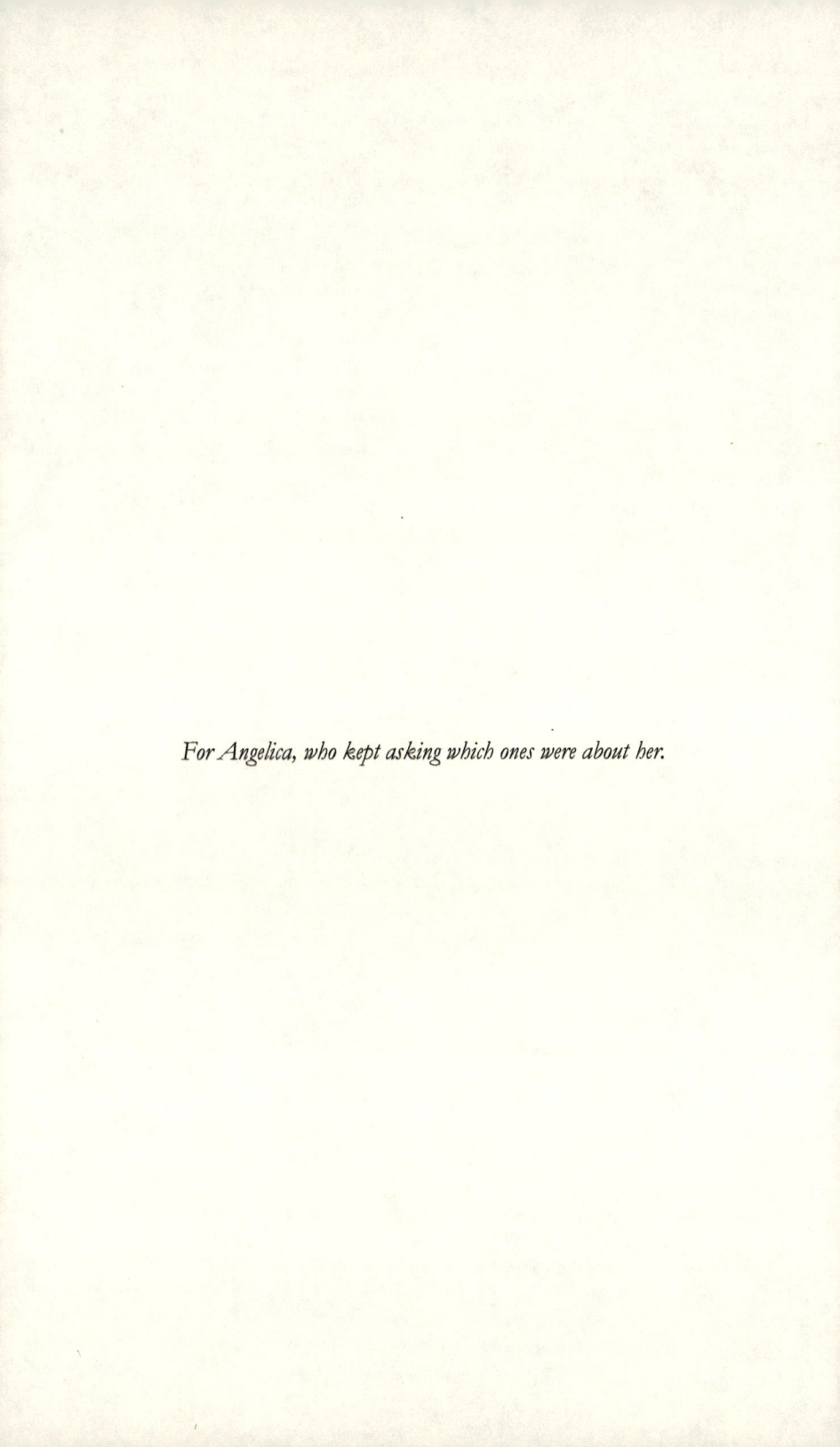

For Angelica, who kept asking which ones were about her.

CONTENTS

INTRODUCTION

Writing a short story a week for a year, that was the challenge I set myself in 2016. The stories had to be no more than 1500 words and they could not be connected in any way to other worlds or characters I had created. Once written, I would publish them on my website, Circumambient Scenery, for the world to see.

Why did I decide to do this?

It's not simply that I enjoy torturing myself with arbitrary challenges that inevitably end in tears and disappointment, at one's basic inability to follow through on anything and the sure knowledge that failure (and ultimately death) awaits us all. That gets me through the night, as I'm sure it does everyone else, but that couldn't be all this was about.

I wanted to push myself as writer. I felt I had become too complacent in some ways and I wanted to see if I could challenge myself. To force myself to write things that I might not otherwise. Whether this was a genre or a style I didn't normally write in, or a tense, tone or perspective I didn't normally adopt, I wanted to see what would happen if I didn't do what came naturally.

I also wanted to see if I could get myself to write with more brevity, and what better way to do that than to force concision upon myself with a word limit. Practice is not something people often talk about with regards to writing, but that was a fundamental part of this challenge. If I made myself write a short story a week, with a strict (kind of) word limit, by the end of the year, I should have a better idea of how to write with concision and focus. That was the theory anyway.

Along those same lines, I also wanted to get better at writing when I had no inspiration and no ideas of what to write. Muses are fickle, tedious creatures in my experience, not to be relied upon. As a result, the majority of these stories began with a blank page and no sense at all of what I was going to write about that week. I began with a sentence and then another and let my mind take me where it wanted to go.

Finally, and most importantly, I wanted to have fun. Writing, is a pleasurable exercise. At least I think it should be. But, like anything else, it can grow stale if you keep doing the same thing over and over. By starting fresh each week, I ensured that I was always doing going down new and different paths.

The stories that resulted from that challenge I set for myself are collected here. The mathematically inclined will note there are more than 52 stories here. In order to give myself a bit of a cushion for the inevitable weeks when I was unable to finish a story (I somehow always managed to get something started), I started writing a month early.

As expected, there were a few failures. There were trips to Machu Picchu. Sickness. Health. Miscreant geese. Recalcitrant alpacas. 1500 word stories morphed into a multi-volume book series. The usual run of life, in other words. But I also managed a few weeks where I got more than one story written, with the end result that I ended with more than the 52 stories I had planned.

It should also be noted that not all them adhere strictly to the 1500 word limit I initially set, although those that do exceed that limit, do so by no more than a hundred or so words. I have left them at the length I think they work best. They are failures, in a sense, but failure is bracing in measured doses. Like the cold embrace of winter, but before the frostbite and hypothermia arrive.

As I write this, having successfully completed 52 plus weeks of writing short stories, I can say that I succeeded in meeting all the goals I had when I set out. The merits of the stories themselves, I will leave to the readers to judge. I know that I enjoyed writing them all, and I hope that you enjoy reading them.

WAYS OF THE HEART

THE FLITCRAFT EFFECT

Musaira Deshu lived an unremarkable life as such things were measured. She worked for a company that provided the processed food and other supplies for several planetary and asteroid mining conglomerates. When she was introduced to people they invariably commented on how interesting her job must be, associated with such interstellar daring. Space travel, with all its attendant consequences, was still a novelty for most people, who would never so much as think of leaving the planet surface, except to visit a thermospheric resort.

Musaira was in fact one of these. Her job was in payroll and compliance. The closest she came to space was when she calculated the taxable benefits for those off planet, who had different exemptions than those on. She was completely fine with this. The job was not what one would call exciting, but she took satisfaction in it and considered herself quite good at it. She was married and had a young daughter, and much of the joy she found in life came there.

One day, on her way to work, she was nearly hit by a falling pane of glass as she walked by a tower that was under construction. Workers had been installing the windows above and had left one resting against the ledge on the roof. Somehow a gust of wind caught it, lifted it up, and sent it tumbling down to the ground. The police, when they investigated, said it was just poor luck that it had happened, though they expected the construction company to be fined for failing to take the necessary precautions.

For Musaira the incident was a revelation. The glass landed right beside her as she walked by the tower. She could feel the brush of the wind as it passed by, and had actually looked to see if someone was reaching out to get her attention. She turned in time to see the glass shatter and let out a scream, jumping back. In spite of the shards of glass spraying in all directions around her, she wound up with only a small cut on her left hand. People farther away than her ended up with cuts and bits of glass embedded in their flesh. One man even lost an eye.

It was extraordinary, Musaira thought. How could she have come so near to dying and yet escape untouched? People said it was luck, a sign, or providence. She felt it was all those things and more. As she walked into work after filling in the police reports, she decided then and there what she would do. She went to one of the recruiters who worked in her office and asked him to sign her up for the longest duration voyage available.

He was dumbfounded by her request. "Your husband will be dead by the time you get back. Your daughter might be too."

She would not be dissuaded. All the psych evals came back normal and the conglomerate happily agreed to sign her up for training. There were limited numbers of people willing to sacrifice the entirety of the lives they had built on a glorified supply run through space. Many of her colleagues were concerned about her, wondering what could possibly have inspired what they saw as a rash and horrific decision. They did little to intervene, assuming that once the tedium of the two months of training set in and she had time to think further on the enormity of what she was doing, she would change her mind.

Musaira did not though, and when the day of the ship launch came she said goodbye to her still disbelieving husband and her daughter—who at three was too young to comprehend what was happening—and went to the launch pad. The other astronauts had friends and family there to say their goodbyes, but all of hers had stayed away, uncomfortable with the seemingly unbelievable decision she had made. But as she stepped aboard and strapped herself into her chair for the launch, Musaira felt no regrets. Her entire being vibrated with joy at the universe that lay before her.

The journey to the asteroid being mined at the edges of the solar system and back to the planet took nearly six years of her time to complete, enough time that the sharp excitement and newness of each day gradually wore smooth, until it was neither exciting, nor interesting, but simply existence as it was. They encountered few problems, completing the mission as intended, and returned to the planet without fanfare or celebration.

Musaira though felt an immense satisfaction at all she had dared and accomplished. She regretted nothing, though now she felt she might like to remain upon the planet and carry on with her life there. Seventy years had passed in the time she had been in space. Her husband had died, after marrying another woman and having two more children. Her daughter had gone on with her life as well, though Musaira was reluctant to investigate too much, not wanting to interfere with her new existence.

Instead she resumed her old position in payroll and compliance with the conglomerate. All her old colleagues had long since retired and there had been changes so vast that she found it disorienting simply to walk down the street. She was now a person out of time, unfamiliar with the most basic of cultural references and shorthand everyone took for granted. After a year back on the planet she shipped out again, this time on a vessel that would be gone for ten years.

When she returned home after that journey she was nearing fifty and was too old for the conglomerate to consider for other voyages. She had made more than enough money to last her for the rest of her life, and so she decided to retire to a tropical island and spend what time remained to her there. She bought a small hotel and ran it, settling into the routine of these new days. A widower came to stay for a week and ended up not leaving. After two months he moved out of his room and permanently into her apartments. Ten years passed in an instant and she felt as though she had never been anywhere else.

One day a woman, in her late thirties, arrived and stayed for a week. She was reserved but pleasant and Musaira felt certain that she knew her, though that was obviously impossible. Everyone she had known in her past lifetimes was long dead, and everyone she knew now was here.

The woman caught her staring at her at breakfast one day and said, "You don't recognize me at all do you?"

Musaira shook her head.

"I don't know how many lifetimes I've waited for this moment."

Musaira nodded, understanding at last. "More than most I would imagine."

LOVE CONQUERS ALL

One of us has to write if anything's to be said. It is a fool's game even in our most lucid moments of passage. Better to admit that we are feeble, tired and pathetic things, no matter where we stand, no matter how time happens to sift. But maybe, maybe I can speak the words to make it stand still.

You tie me in knots, still and almost latent, hushed with anticipation and the heavy weight of knowing. You are the breath of morning sunshine upon my face. Your eyes are like quicksilver to my bloodstream. The Spanish will declare a monopoly on that careless glance, sending ships across the ocean, peering steadily beyond the waves. They will desire conquest and ruin, claiming you for all time.

I want to steal but a moment and make it eternal. As you brush the hair from your eyes, those stray glancing strands, they whisper and I remember what they are saying about the nature of eternity. Eternity is not forever, it just feels that way, if you're lucky.

The violence of a single moment is startling. It overwhelms the senses, leaves you breathless with fear and wonder. The rain pours and then dries slowly away as the sun emerges. How surreal to be separated from the cataclysm, standing and watching in a passing thought, empty of everything. I never felt the lightning, only heard the echo of thunder long after the blinding flash had turned my eyes to dust.

I need a shot of salvation, a taste of the sacrosanct, to get me through the ends of the day. Those moments when you're left with only yourself to feel pitiful about are the worst, the need of a soul laid bare for everyone to see. Survival's the thing people find difficult, convinced of the betrayal of existence.

Western Swing on the transistor: cried for you, cried a while, wandering like a river and the rain don't stop. The deluge of the moment that doesn't quite cut clean, that doesn't ever quite end. The mess of things you just can't escape. Like the tangle of our bodies, it never had that sort of finality. Life is unexpected, unready as we are.

I wonder if we ever really learn anything as the years drift by, or if we stay rooted in these places we were before, grown so thick and full in sunlight. Now they are cast in shadows and tremors of moments you hesitate to come to. I remember, with the darkness of a long night, those sudden stunning instants of time, of universe, of whatever it is we might be, when I felt like I could understand.

But these things they get away from you, and the cosmos feels irreparably empty. Your shining eyes, your moistened lips, once, once I drank you in. And now to stand here. These words mean nothing, but I will say them all the same.

AN AFTERNOON SHOWER IN THE CITY

The first spatter of rain hit Aada on the arm as she walked down 35th Avenue. She grimaced and looked up at the sky where ominous clouds were gathering. The first signs of the coming storm had been there when she ducked out of her apartment to run a few errands, but she had hoped to beat its arrival—the grocery store and bakery were only ten minutes away after all. Now, her arms heavy with full bags, she faced the prospect of a downpour, or worse.

It was only a little more than five blocks to her apartment, but she had no umbrella and could not run, loaded down with groceries as she was. And she did not want them, or the contents of her purse, to get soaked. The rain started, a few drops here and there splattering down, and she told herself that maybe this was all it would amount to. Even as she was thinking it, the drops turned into cascades of water and she drenched. She saw a flash of lightning on the horizon and heard a low rumble of thunder in response.

A few white pellets of hail bounced off the pavement as well, telling her that things could very quickly turn ugly if she did not find some sort of cover. She cast about and saw that she had just passed a three story building that had a short awning extending out over the stairs leading up to its entrance. "That'll do," she said to herself and ran, as best she could, toward it.

It was only once she was up the stairs and at the building door that she saw she was not alone. A man stood in the corner of the entryway, leaning beside the intercom, staring out at the falling rain. He straightened as she came up the stairs, and gestured to the buzzer. "You need this?"

She shook her head, her long damp hair flapping into her eyes. "Thanks," she said, as she set her grocery bags on the steps.

As Aada straightened up, turning to look out at the descending rain, she could feel the guy's eyes upon her. She was suddenly conscious of the fact that her clothes were soaked, the t-shirt she was wearing now accentuating her form more than she was comfortable. Pushing aside the sinking feeling in her stomach, she shot the man a quick glare, and set her expression at what she hoped was a solid, *don't fuck with me* kind of indifference.

"Hell of a shower," the guy said, his voice low and barely audible over the crescendo of the rain. "Sucks to get caught out with groceries too."

Oh great, Aada thought. "Yeah," she said, giving him the barest of nods, not taking her gaze off the street.

They both watched as a cyclist raced by, head bent over into the face of the rain. A couple passed, arms around each other under an umbrella, instinctively ducking at the next crash of thunder.

The guy exhaled, whether from nerves or boredom, and Aada had to resist a smile. She resolved not to look in his direction and was soon overwhelmed by the need to do so.

For Christsakes.

He had a beard and dark eyes, both notorious weaknesses of hers. But there was also the fact that, to judge by his too-stylish clothes and his overly made up hair, he was an insufferable prick. He was good looking though, a fact she wanted desperately to confirm again, but which she would not allow herself to do. Bad enough to be stuck here, no sense encouraging him.

Aada sensed before he spoke that he was gearing up to try again. "You live around here, I guess?"

She looked down at her grocery bags and over at him, giving him a withering look.

"Yeah," the guy said, turning to look out at the street, resisting his own rueful smile.

At least he understood how sorry an excuse for chatting her up this was. It was almost enough for her to think about taking pity on him. Almost.

They watched the storm in silence for a time, both flinching at the lightning sparking across the clouds. The rain showed no signs of abating, but the guy seemed to have given up, deciding the modest amount of embarrassment he had suffered was enough for the day. For that, Aada was glad and she began to relax, forgetting about the guy and starting to craft the story she would tell her friends about this incident when she next saw them.

The rain seemed to ebb for a moment, tricking her into thinking it was nearing its end, when the door to the apartment building opened behind her. A man in a ballcap and electric yellow shorts stepped out and squinted at Aada and the guy, surprised to see them there. He hesitated, as if he was thinking about saying something, before deciding not to and heading down the steps.

As he stepped onto the sidewalk, and out from under the cover of the awning, he gave a start, as though he had received a shock, and jumped back under cover. He looked around, doing a full 180 of the street and the storm. As he did so, the rain began to fall even heavier than it had before, the drops hitting the pavement so hard they could see them bouncing. The man had seen enough. He retreated back up the steps, unlocking the door and slipping back into the building without looking at either of them.

Aada stared after him as he disappeared around the corner of the lobby. The guy was doing the same thing and he caught her eye and shook his head.

"He didn't just..." Aada said. *What are you doing you damn fool?*

The guy shook his head, peering into the lobby again. "He had no fucking clue it was raining. How is that even possible?"

"I don't know," Aada said. "I mean..." She gestured at the streets, her voice sounding muffled to her own ears with the cacophony of the rain.

As if to emphasize her point, thunder reverberated above them, sounding like an explosion. They both laughed.

"That was amazing," the guy said, smiling at her.

In spite of herself, Aada smiled back at him. He had a good smile. *Goddammit,* she said to herself. Aloud, she said, "My name's Aada."

THE PRINCE AND THE UNICORN

When the Prince of the Seventh Sea and the Lands Beyond the Far Isthmus of Shadows was born, people throughout the realm celebrated. The feasts and celebrations lasted eight days, for the King was considered one of the wisest to ever to rule in those lands, and the people knew that he would raise a son who was just and fair. The King and Queen wept upon seeing the child for the first time, for they had suffered many tribulations in their efforts to have children and they had never seen a baby so beautiful.

That beautiful baby grew into a handsome youth, whose smile seemed to set the birds in the trees to song and make calm the wildest of beasts. He was a brilliant student, and his father spared no expense in bringing tutors from beyond the far reaches of the kingdom, so that the Prince might learn all there was to know of the world. As he grew older, the Prince also became renowned for his exploits. He ran the fastest, climbed the highest, leapt the farthest, and, in general, bested all his companions in whatever game they played.

All in all, the Prince seemed extraordinary, with everyone agreeing that he possessed all the necessary abilities to be a fine King.

When he came of age, his father told him it was time to find a bride and said he could choose any woman in the land. Word was sent out across the realm, even into the depths of the Isthmus of Shadows, that the Prince would receive any lady who would consent to be his wife.

The response from all the subjects in the land was overwhelming. Everyone, whether high or low born, thought their daughter the most beautiful, suitable woman for the perfect prince. They set out for the capital, by carriage, horseback or on foot, no matter how arduous or expensive the journey might be, all determined to stand before the Prince and be found worthy of his love. They lined up by the thousands, from the great halls of the palace down the streets of the city and out the city walls, waiting days upon days for their opportunity.

The Prince received them all, sparing no time for any of his other pursuits, for he understood the sacrifices so many had made to see him. For every woman that curtsied before him he had a kind word and a smile, sometimes even a joke. His questions were always pertinent, but never too inquiring, the conversations neither too long, nor too short. He had a gift for setting all the women at ease and sending them away without disappointment, even if they had failed in their quest.

And fail they did. Woman after woman came before him, and woman after woman he sent away. The King began to grow worried. He went to his son and declared, "All the women of the land have come before you and you find them all lacking. The most beautiful, the most intelligent, the most accomplished woman, you have sent them all away."

"I have not seen the woman I will marry," the Prince said.

"What can you possibly be looking for? You have seen all the realm has to offer."

"I don't know," the Prince said. "All I know is that I haven't seen her yet. When I do, I know she will be the one I will marry."

The King was exasperated, but he said no more. He understood what his son was looking for and he did not have the heart to tell him he would not be able to find it. For it was perfection itself that he sought. It was impossible, but the King knew he would have to learn that for himself.

But the Prince continued to send women away, finding all of them lacking for one reason or another. Unrest began to grow in the capital and across the kingdom, as the populace began to wonder why their Prince should find fault in all of their daughters. The King and Queen pleaded for patience, even as they demanded that their son choose a wife before the people turned against them.

"When I see her I will know," was all he would say.

As the days went on, the lines finally began to dwindle, until some days there were only one or two women for the Prince to see, or none at all. The King became desperate, telling his son that he should choose from one of the women he had already seen. "There are so many fine ladies that you have seen, surely one of them is worthy to be your wife."

The Prince would not be dissuaded though. "I will know her when I see her."

One day, as evening came on and the gates of the city were about to be locked, a woman arrived and asked to see the Prince. There had been no women to see him for two days and it took some time for the courtiers to locate him in the palace and bring him to the great hall so he could receive this claimant. The Prince was weary after a day of jousting and he almost had the courtiers tell the woman to return the next day, that he was too tired to receive her. But he decided that would be impolite and so he summoned what energy remained to him and went to receive her.

As soon as he laid eyes upon her, the Prince knew she was the woman he would marry. "My lady," he said. "You are enchanting."

She curtsied gravely before him. "You are as well, my lord." She glanced around the great hall with some curiosity.

"May I ask where you are from, my lady?" The Prince could barely find the words to say. His face reddened.

"I come from a place beyond the mountains, beyond the sea and beyond the isthmus."

"You are not of this realm? What has brought you here?"

The woman considered the Prince and he felt the smallest person in the world. "I wanted to see what it was like to stand before a Prince in a palace such as this."

The Prince was taken aback at her answer, but he did not dwell on it long, so overwhelming was his passion for this impossibly beautiful woman. "My lady, as I am sure you know, I have been seeking a wife. All the women of these lands have been attending to me so that I might choose one of them to be my bride. Having set eyes upon you, I cannot imagine wedding another. Will you do me the honor of being my wife?"

The woman considered his request for a moment, looking somewhat confused. "I cannot," she said. "I cannot stay among you."

The Prince was wounded deeply, but he covered his hurt as best he could. "I am sorry to hear it, my lady. Perhaps I can convince you to remain with us here awhile. I hope you will enjoy our hospitality."

To the Prince's relief, the woman agreed and quarters were found for her. The Prince spent the next days wooing her, attempting to dazzle her with feats of wit and strength, though nothing seemed to impress her. The woman seemed utterly mystified by his entreaties and indifferent to his feats. The Prince was left heartbroken and inconsolable. Nothing the King or Queen said could rally his spirits.

The Prince was contemplating throwing himself before the woman once more, declaring his undying affection and begging her to be his wife, when word came she had disappeared. He swore immediately that he would not rest until he had found her. He rode across the realm, beyond the mountains, beyond the sea and beyond the isthmus. Once there, he found the lands utterly empty of people and set off into a forest in the hopes of locating anyone who might tell him where the woman who had so possessed might be.

In a clearing in the forest he came across a unicorn, a beast long thought to be myth. But here it was, staring directly at him. Something about its gaze made him pause and he stared back at it, and was filled with the certainty that somehow this unicorn was the beauty who had called upon him in the palace. He got down from his horse and knelt before the creature and said, "I beg of you, come with me and be my wife. I will do whatever to make you happy."

The unicorn did not say anything, but still the Prince came to know its answer. He nodded, tears stinging his eyes, and rode home. Though the King and Queen begged him to reconsider the Prince never married, for he was convinced no woman in the land could match the one who had been a unicorn. Even after his parents died and he came to the throne, Prince refused to marry any woman and he bore no children. He ruled as wisely and justly as his father had, but after he died the land fell to ruin.

THE ADVENTURES OF HOLLY AND MORRIS

They hit the payroll, catching them in a crossfire as they came into Horseshoe Canyon on their way to pay the miners at the Atlas Coal Mine in Wayne. There were only two guns protecting it and Morris and Holly picked one off each from their perches across the canyon. The two men leading the packhorses tried to flee, but they shot the horses out from under them and then had to scramble to their own mounts to catch up with the fleeing payroll. That they did, intercepting the stampeding horses before they could scamper up the narrow and winding trail that led from the canyon to the plains above.

When they had calmed the panicked animals they left the canyon behind, heading up into the hills to the north where they had a camp set up. There they watered the horses and set them loose to eat and counted their day's earnings. They were giddy as they went through the coins and the well-creased bills, over two hundred fifty dollars worth. They could sell the two pack horses too and probably get close to three hundred when it was all said and done. Holly whooped and danced, kissing Morris and pulling at his beard.

He laughed in joy at her delight. "No more worries for awhile, Holly dear."

"No more worries, Morris honey," she said and pulled him to his feet to join in her dance.

Once they had eaten and the horses had rested they set off again, having transferred the payroll to their person and gotten rid of the satchels. They rode east into ranching country, pressing as far as they thought the horses could manage, before setting up camp for the night. A fire seemed risky so they ate pemmican they had made some days before and fell into each other's arms for warmth. Coyotes and foxes provided a chorus as they drifted off to sleep.

The next morning they were on horseback before dawn, setting a hard pace. When they came near to Brooks, Morris headed into the town and sold the two pack horses, leaving Holly to wait on the outskirts of town. An hour later a posse arrived by train, led by the Northwest Mounted Police. They interviewed the locals and found the man who Morris had sold the horses to, which matched the description of a man whose face could be seen in every post office in the territory.

Everyone they talked to agreed, Morris Hestin had left town heading east and so that was the way the posse went. The posse's scout picked up their trail and they followed it for two days. It was on the evening of the first that Morris and Holly caught wind of the pursuit and decided to ride all night to see if they could lose them. The posse was relentless, though, and had fresher horses and no need to press them, confident in their scout's abilities. On the evening of the second day the scout took them into the Cypress Hills.

Morris and Holly had taken refuge in a trapper's cabin in the forest surrounding Elkwater Lake. Set atop a hill they reasoned they would have a clear view of anyone approaching, and if necessary they could make their escape down one of the trapper's trails. They had food and water to last another two or three days before they would have to flee. But they had not anticipated a posse in pursuit, expecting there to be only a handful of men, not the dozen or more who arrived at the foot of the hill on the morning of the third day.

When Morris saw the number of men gathered below, peering up at the trapper's shack, he knew they had little time to waste. He roused Holly from her slumber and led her at a run out the back of the cabin to one the trails, hoping the posse hadn't had time to discover them all. They left the horses behind at the front of the cabin, hoping to slip through the posse's net before they even realized the two had gone.

They almost made it, but one of the posse, a young man with a burnt face, caught sight of someone ducking around the cabin to the trails. The posse split, with half of them rushing up the hill in pursuit, while the other half moved around the hill, trying to cut off their escape trail. Morris and Holly fled, careening down one of the trails. Behind them they could hear the sounds of the posse in pursuit, the thunder of the hooves on the hilltop.

"We got to get where there horses can't go," Morris said, between frantic breaths. Molly just nodded and they dove off the trail and into the forest where the underbrush was thickest.

The two arms of the posse met up half an hour later and they realized that somehow Morris and his counterpart had made their escape. A few rushed back to the trapper's cabin to make sure the two didn't return for their horses, while the rest got off their horses and combed through the trees, trying to pick up their trail. By the time they did, Morris and Holly had stolen a couple of horses from an American whiskey trader—who the posse found dead the next day, his throat slashed—and they were on the run again.

It was not until two weeks later that the posse picked up their trail again, which led them to Dorothy, a little village not far from Wayne and East Coulee where the robbery had taken place. The NWMP men removed their uniforms and trickled into town slowly over the morning, so as not to alert Morris and his counterpart. A few words with the locals revealed that Morris was in the Dorothy Hotel where he had taken up with a woman for the last two days. The Mounties agreed that he and his counterpart must have parted ways at some point since the Cypress Hills.

The constable in charge of the posse slipped into the hotel to talk with the manager, who confirmed everything. "Yep, those two came in together day before last. Hardly seen 'em since. They get food and drink sent up there. Not stingy, by any means."

There was no one else staying in the rooms on the top floor, so the constable had the rest hotel evacuated while his men surround the building. They put men on the stairs, men on the fire escape, men at each exit, and on every street surrounding the hotel. The constable and two other men went up the stairs and down the hall to the room where Morris and his woman were cooped up.

"Morris Hestin," the constable called out, as he came near the door. "We know you're in there. We have the building surrounded. Surrender now."

There was no response within, though the constable could hear a flurry of movement, including what sounded like a pistol being cocked. "Don't be a damn fool Morris. You can't shoot your way out of this." The constable paused and looked at the nervous faces with him in the hallway. "At least send the girl out. She's no part of this."

Within the room Morris was peering out the curtains of the window. "Looks like we're through Holly dear."

"No, Morris, no. There's always a way." There were tears in Holly's voice and on her face.

Morris turned back to her and gave a sad shake of his head. "I'm sorry Holly. But there's no way out for me. You can go though."

"I won't leave you Morris."

"There's no sense both of us getting hanged Holly. No sense at all. You heard the man. They don't know you was a part of it. You can walk right on out of here. So you just go. Leave some of the money and just go."

Holly shook her head, tears streaming down her cheeks. "I won't leave you Morris. Not like this."

"You got to Holly. You got to."

At last Holly nodded. She gathered most of the money, hiding it on her person, and pulled out her pistol and shot Morris in the heart.

"I got him," she called out. "I got his gun and I shot him."

She threw the pistol on the floor and held up her hands, watching as Morris slid down, his hands at his chest. The constable burst into the room with the others behind him, their own pistols raised. Morris looked up at them and then found Holly's eyes and he smiled.

HOW TO MAKE LOVE LIKE A WARLOCK

Although many exhaustive and learned volumes have been published on the subject of amorous instruction, I feel much remains to be said on the matter, especially as it pertains to the copulatory habits of warlocks and other masters of dark magic. As one well-practiced in both infernal arts, I feel well suited to speak on the matter with the clarity required, lest another poor apprentice or sorcerer be led astray into more dismal and dreary acts, for lack of knowledge on how to properly engage with an enchantress, siren or familiar.

Firstly, one must attach the suitable appendage. On acquiring the requisite appendage, I will say little now, though it perhaps warrants its own appendix, for it is a matter worthy of careful consideration. Many is the dark master who endeavors to perform the salacious act, only to find his chosen member shriveled and smelling of putrescence. No amount of ointment or potion will see you to satisfying either party in that situation.

The subject puts me in mind of a story, which if the reader will allow me the indulgence of a small digression, I will detail here. I was in a cemetery practicing a poor bit of necromancy—never one of my finer talents, I am sorry to admit—when I came across a sorcerer collecting mandrake root. I was cold and damp from my evening's toil, and glad for the company, so I shared some of my tobacco and we each drew on our pipes.

After explaining that I had been engaged to summon the recalcitrant spirit of a distant father by a spurned son, cast out of inheritance, I inquired as to what had brought him to this place. "I am collecting the female of the mandrake root," he said, with a gesture to his satchel.

"To what end?" I said, for I was curious as to what spell he was conducting. As anyone familiar with the arts will be aware, there are many uses for the mandrake root, both male and female.

"I am effecting a spell of transformation," the sorcerer said, somewhat guardedly.

"I am quite familiar with the endeavor," I told him enthusiastically. "Who is undergoing the transformation?"

"That would be me," the sorcerer said, after a moment in which he looked away longingly into the darkness.

Seeing an opportunity, I offered to assist the young man in his deed. He could utilize my experience and skill in effecting a successful transformation, and in return I would receive what was sloughed off in the process for my own personal use. The lesson, as always, help those who trod this dark path with you and you will be repaid with bounties unimaginable.

To return to my purpose though: while the proper appendage is, of course, essential, it by no means assures success in the act, despite what many will boastfully claim. From the crypt to the necropolis to the haunted forest, and along every nefarious byway that our feet shall trod upon, one must always bring all one's skills to bear upon the situation. Perhaps this is an ancient spell or curse, a potion or concoction made of bitterroot and poison, an ensorcelled mirror or blade, or an enslaved imp or demon. All of these will add pleasure to the task at hand. Use them judiciously, though, for there is nothing worse to have your coitus interrupted by an enraged goblin, slipped free of the bonds that held him, taking possession of the dagger you imbued with dark powers. One would be lucky to escape with possession of all ones appendages. As the reader may already have surmised, I speak from sad experience.

In all things, variety is the newt eye of the potion. Perhaps you delight in excoriation of a maiden pure. However, do not limit your acts to only those practices, for soon they will become rituals and these tend toward the hidebound. You will become as rote and dreary as the Church, which condemns us and seeks our destruction. We are governed by no one, except the dark arts we study. Let no one forget!

An example might serve to best explicate my meaning, so I will endeavor to provide one from my own experience, in the hopes that it will provide you with some use in your own practices. I once was familiar with a woman, learned in many dark matters, who took great delight in cuckolding her husband. Her greatest desire, beyond the pleasure of the act and the knowledge that she was thwarting her husband, lay in her husband discovering her just as she reached the climax of her pleasure. I, naturally, wished to see to the dark lady's notorious desires, but without incurring the wrath of her husband while engaged in the profane act. I had a certain degree of experience in the matter, and I well knew such interruptions were not only inopportune, they often resulted in considerable injury, something I wished to avoid.

A happy compromise presented itself, one that would satisfy both the lady's considerable desire and my own preference to keep all my appendages safely intact. I bespelled an imp, a terribly vicious creature, who happened also to be an excellent mimic of an individual's voice and speech. I stuffed him in an empty ale cask which I, in the guise of a mere peasant, delivered to the lady's home. She delighted in my subterfuge and quickly we fell to our infernal task. As her pleasure reached its natural crescendo, I compelled the imp to speak in her husband's voice and so led her to a greater satisfaction than she had previously known.

After, when it became evident that her husband was not going to materialize demanding explanations and a pound of my flesh, she demanded one of her own. Though I resisted stridently, she managed to draw the secret from me and I revealed the imp and had him display his remarkable talent. Once it had been demonstrated, the imp became an integral part of our assignations, as I soon came to regret. For there came a point where the lady reached the conclusion that the imp was far more integral than I to the proceedings, and she released me from my duties while claiming him to see the task done.

Such are the vagaries of the amorous life. It is forever instructive, even as it frustrates and leads one to despair. But if my task here is well completed, I will hopefully spare the careful reader some manner of frustration that I have endured and save him or her from misery. But, I must beg the faithful reader's forgiveness, for I must put pen aside for the moment and retreat from my study. I hear my dark mistress's terrible call and I must see to the satiation of her infernal desires.

ONLY LOVE CAN BREAK YOUR HEART

"Hi. Anjali?" A lopsided grin and uncomfortable eyes.

"Yes," she says, her own eyes downcast, but taking him in all the same. "You must be Ryland."

"That's right."

A pause, both of them waiting for the other to speak. They both start at the same time and stop together, wincing.

"Shall we?" Ryland says, gesturing and gulping for air.

Anjali nods and leads the way to the nearest table. They sit across from each other, taking the measure of the situation. A buzz of conversation settles over them, reminding each of them of their own silence. They look away at others, trying to ignore the awkwardness.

A waitress flits by and smiles conspiratorially. "How are you guys tonight? Can I get you started with some drinks?"

Relief. They order. He gets a beer and she has a mojito. The waitress nods, pleased by their choices and disappears. Ryland watches her go, before reminding himself not to and turns his attention back to Anjali.

"So, how was your day?" he says with an attempt at joviality. He winces at the sound and hopes she doesn't notice.

Anjali suppresses her own grimace. *These same damn questions.* "I'm just glad it's the end of the week."

"Any big plans?" Ryland says, not wanting to lose the momentum he feels he has started.

Anjali shrugs, knowing she can't say she will most likely spend the day on the couch in her pajamas watching Criminal Minds reruns. "I'm just getting together with some friends." A safe, non-specific lie. "What about you?"

"Not too much planned," Ryland says, considering and rejecting several possible answers, none of which involve him staying up until two in the morning playing video games and drinking beer with his roommate. "I was thinking of going on a bike ride on Sunday."

The waitress arrives with their drinks and asks if they would like food. The both decline and she leaves them alone. Anjali asks about where he likes to go biking and he provides an overly long, detailed answer that he knows is utterly boring her and yet he cannot stop himself from seeing through to its end. He asks her what she likes to do for fun and she tells him something.

God this awkward, she thinks. *This isn't going as badly as I thought,* he thinks.

The waitress returns when they are both near the bottom of their drinks. Ryland orders another and Anjali declines and asks for a water. The conversation slowly dwindles until they lapse into silence, staring past each other at the rest of the bar.

"What do you think is going on over there?" Anjali says, as Ryland frantically tries to think of something, anything to say to spark the conversation again.

Ryland turns around to look upon his saviors and sees an old woman sitting alone at a table with a half empty pint of beer and a leopard print purse upon it. Their waitress stops by her table and they chat for a bit, the old woman saying something that makes the server laugh.

"She does seem a bit old for this crowd," Ryland says. "But then I do too."

"God, I know, right. I keep thinking I should tell our waitress to card the kids at the next table. There's no way they're nineteen."

"I've been coming here since I was in university," Ryland says, "and I feel like Matthew McConaghey in Dazed and Confused. I keep getting older and everyone else is staying the same age."

"I know what you mean," Anjali says. "I hope I can be as badass as she is and still go into places like this when I'm her age."

They both look at the woman again. The waitress comes by to check on them, and follows their gaze. "You guys like Deborah? She's quite the lady."

"Does she come here often?" Anjali says.

"Once or twice a week. She has a pint or two and then goes out for supper. Tonight she told me she has a gentleman caller."

"Oh my god," Ryland says laughing. "Did she actually say gentleman caller?"

"She did," the waitress says.

"Amazing."

"Yeah," Anjali says. "You know what, I think I will have another mojito."

Ryland smiles. "And her second pint is on me," he says.

Both their gazes linger on the woman a moment longer as the waitress leaves, before they turn back. Their eyes meet and they start again.

BLOSSOMING HEARTS

In springtime the nobles of Nazagul would gather in the finer districts of the city, or, for those of particular fortune, in the court of the Emperor himself, to watch the blossoming of the baha flowers. Such an occasion, which came but once a year and lasted for only a week—two if the season was truly favorable—was an opportunity to observe the ephemeral splendor of nature. Life itself was transient and fleeting, a moment that passed and disappeared without a thought. A beauty that could never be captured and held.

Genha felt herself to be in such a moment now, an exquisite perfection that she would spend the rest of her days seeking to replicate, all to no avail. Everything stood on the precipice ready to collapse, but it yet stood, all in balance. The flowers bloomed, and though she knew the day would come, not long from now, when the blossoms would fall and scatter to the winds, they seemed so alive that she could almost believe it was impossible that they should perish.

The moment of her realization came during that year's baha festivities. She and her husband attended the celebration of one of the Emperor's viziers in the hills above the imperial city in the park the Emperor had set aside for the nobility. The group of them— the vizier and his wife, Genha and her husband, their children and retainers—sat beneath one of the baha trees, five trees from the Emperor himself. Two trees further yet was the family Leiy's celebration, and sitting with them was their firstborn son and his wife and their children.

They spent the afternoon beneath the trees contemplating the baha blossoms, amidst laughter and joking , eating and drinking,. The moment that Genha would remember, that she would treasure for the remainder of her days, came as the sun's descent became obvious. The shadow's began to lengthen around them, the air seeming to change, as if to announce that night would not be held at bay for long. As she sat at the edge of the vizier's blanket, watching her second-born son play with the vizier's firstborn daughter, she felt the eyes of someone upon her and glanced up to see the Firstborn Leiy staring at her. Their eyes met for an instant, and they both looked away before anyone noticed. It was in that instant, that exquisite glance, that Genha realized she had never known such happiness.

The day went on and the blankets were folded up and the Emperor led the procession back into the imperial city. As they descended from the hills, down the wide imperial avenue, everyone could see as smoke began to billow from the Xavin District near the city walls. A quiet murmur passed through the crowd, as various parties speculated about the fire and its cause, as well as its location, so near the army barracks. The Emperor made no comment and gave no sign he even noticed the blaze, leading the procession below with his head held high.

The fires turned out to be far more serious than even the most pessimistic might have ventured on that day. They were but one of many fires at imperial buildings throughout the land. An uprising against the Emperor had begun. The viziers, and many other important nobles, were summoned to discuss the matter, including Genha's husband. More importantly for Genha, so was the Firstborn Leiy. She felt his absence keenly in those first days of the rebellion, when the advisers argued throughout the day and deep into the night.

At the height of her longing for him, on the second day of the meetings at the palace, a messenger arrived with a poem from the Firstborn Leiy. In it he expressed his own unreserved delight at their shared glance, comparing the cataclysms in his heart at that moment to the ones that now threatened to consume the empire. It was a scandalous poem, with it's suggestion that their affair could be equated in any way with the struggle to overthrow the Emperor. To even have it in her possession was a risk to both her and the

Firstborn Leiy, and it thrilled her to no end.

It also proved to be the beginning of the end of this moment of exquisite perfection, whose brief season it seemed had passed. Genha's husband had sent his own messenger that same afternoon with his own unimaginative poem. He arrived just as the Firstborn Leiy's was leaving with her reply. The servant informed her husband, and when he returned home from the palace two days later, he demanded to know what message had been delivered to her. Genha could not produce a message or provide a suitable explanation to allay his fears and so they settled into a period of suspicion and hostility.

The uprising proved to be far more intractable than anyone had anticipated, word arriving soon after the end of the meetings in the palace of certain borderland outposts being overrun and seized. The streets of the imperial city became fraught with tension, the imperial guard on every corner. It became hard to move about the city, though as a noble Genha was granted allowances others less fortunate were not. It only served to heighten the illicitness and the danger of what she was doing with Firstborn Leiy when they met next.

Still, when the fevers of their passion had died they found little to say, the reality of having to traverse the garrisoned city, as well as avoiding her husband's spies, settling upon both of them. Word had come of still further losses in the provinces of the empire and of a gathering force, a consuming whirlwind, that had begun to move toward the imperial city. The Firstborn Leiy had an audience with the Emperor and the rest of his advisers that evening to discuss matters and Genha could sense his thoughts already casting there as they embraced and kissed goodbye.

The news grew only worse in the days that followed. It seemed nothing the Emperor did could quiet the rebellion and his advisers were soon at a loss as to what to say. The Firstborn Leiy sent Genha another poem, but it was hurried and distracted, the matters of the day calling for too much of his attention. She felt the moment slipping away, taken by the wind, even as her ardor for him did not quiet.

That was the world they lived in, she knew, a transient place where heartbreak was the only constant. Celebrations of the baha blossoms were canceled, deemed too dangerous to attend with the unrest growing. Genha spent those last days of the bloom alone in her quarters, remembering that glance and all that had gone with it. It was all over by the time the blossoms were gone.

ALL THAT REMAINS

I emerged, crawling upward from the bowels of unending, the grime thick and the smoke spreading.

What lay there, I hardly recall. My thoughts were not my own then. They are barely my own now. I am not who I am, you see. I am all that remains.

Here is what I remember of that dark time. The memory of that caustic smoke, acrid tasting, stings my eyes still. The dim phosphorescence provided by the braziers stationed on the walls at various junctures left everything shrouded, so that I made my way through the boweled earth by feel as much as by sight. It mattered little for I trod the same path each day, the hours of my waking passing with a regularity that provided its own kind of timekeeping. I knew when to sleep. I knew when to eat. I knew what to do at every moment of every day.

My tasks I barely understood, only that they were ancient and immutable, part of a vast undertaking involving those thousands of us who lived below. I knew nothing of them and they nothing of me. Our existence was tied solely to what duty required of us. Hour after hour, day after day, we moved through those tunnels and byways, in service to those who had gone. Our chants and songs, incantations and prayers, filled the air, clouding it as much as the smoke, never falling silent, easing me to sleep when my time came.

What we did defined us and I remember so little of it now. Every step, every gesture of my hands, every intonation, all so precisely done, in spite of the obscurity we existed in. The meaning of it all escapes me. I am not who I was.

I emerged from the unseen, the blackness of tunnel and the shuddering entrails of labyrinth.

All of us existed as units of a single organism, with a single goal. To service those who had gone. The ones who had passed to the beyond, to the darkness darker than the one we submitted ourselves to. They held more power than we the living did. They could be angry and capricious, these ancient dead, and the caverns and chambers where we intoned our rites were alive with their power. Alive with them, in a way we could never be alive, for we had submitted our lives to them.

I knew nothing of the world beyond the corridors I traversed day after day. There were whispers of what lay above, of realms beyond imagining. They were spoken of in hushed, secretive tones, with glances over the shoulder. To do so was blasphemy. The world above was not ours. We were the dead, in service to them, awaiting our own glory in the beyond.

They held the power there, ancient and immutable. Unspeakable as the stones. We spoke for them, our chants ringing through the darkness, echoing as far as the world above. Or so I imagined.

Began to imagine, I should say. A whisper of a thought formed slowly, a seedling pushing up to the light in a desert, desperate for water and nourishment. It was someone else within me speaking, a ghost trying to breathe life into itself, wheezing on the noxious air it found.

Once a week, at the same junction, on my way to the same stone, deep in the catacombs, I would see the same man. I do not know when it began, but we started to smile at one another, the briefest flash of a grin, there and then gone. If one of us was late in arriving, the other would find an excuse to linger for a moment or two. After a time that smile was transformed to the briefest of touches, one hand to another.

The electricity of that touch, sparked in me my other self. The self that dreamed of the world above, the sky that I had never seen.

One day the man did not appear. Nor was he there the next week, and I began to understand what sorrow was and the futility of our incantations for those who had gone and those who remained.

I emerged, my face blurring, misshapen in form and somehow incomplete.

For the first time, I felt a heart beating in my chest, and the sweetness of the air filling my lungs. I yearned to be free of the rituals that bound me, the empty endless routines that clung to me like so much gathered dust. Such thoughts had never entered my mind before. I had no conception of how to effect an escape. Escape was a novel concept. These catacombs were all I knew. They were as much who I was as the blood that flowed in my veins.

One day I simply walked away, ignoring my duties, the rituals to those who had passed beyond. I could feel their anger at my abandonment, shaking the very stones I passed by. I had no sense of where to go, of what to do, I simply wandered, avoiding the gaze of anyone who looked my way, heading for where the smoke seemed to lessen. By and by I found my way, the bowels becoming less crowded, until I felt the first breeze, cool and crisp, touch my lips.

I emerged, a stumbling figure on a parched landscape. The sky was bright, the ground red, and the silence pervasive.

THE INSPECTORS

The gas giant hid secrets, long buried, or so they hoped. Tlan Garsh and Yzal Bey, the lead inspectors for the Exalted Gerent, who ruled this miserable portion of the galaxy, had come looking for the one who had betrayed him. They had followed a trail, intermittent and well-disguised, and the evidence had brought them here to this abandoned system, with only this massive gas giant left unharvested for resources by the Gerent's Marauders.

For months and months, as the Marauders laid waste to the feeble forces of Sborz system, intending to enslave the population and extract what was usable from its planets and habitats, there had been problems. These had been tiny and insignificant, hardly worth reporting to the Exalted Gerent—though a failure to do so would, if discovered, result in a horrible and inventive punishment. The delays to the Marauders ultimate conquest of the system were minimal, but, all the same, however inconsequential the issue, it had to be resolved.

The Exalted Gerent did not countenance betrayal of any sort, and there could be no doubt that this was a betrayal of his mandate. Tlan and Yzal had established that to everyone's satisfaction. Someone within the ranks of the Marauders, or worse—and this did not really bear thinking about, for the consequences would be dire for anyone even tangentially involved—within the Gerent's inner circle. This was why Tlan and Yzal had been directed, by the Exalted Gerent himself, to find whoever it was who was daring to defy him and see justice done.

Their ship informed them that the system was empty as they passed out of the portal, the only remnant of the worlds that had once existed here. This was to be expected and neither one paid it any mind. Tlan directed the vessel toward the gas giant, the coordinates of which had been broadcast from ships within the Marauder fleet on each occasion when the double agent had sent information to their enemies. The coordinates, they had discovered, contained information packets, cleverly concealed, that revealed the position of the Marauder fleet, it's planned movements, and its numbers, among other things.

The ship ran any number of scans of the gas giant and sent in a few probes. All revealed the same thing: this was gas giant, like any other gas giant. There was nothing remarkable about it.

Tlan looked at Yzal with a wordless question: What now?

Yzal shrugged. "It doesn't make any sense. There's nothing here. And I don't see any connection to Sborz. Or the Marauders."

"Some will have come from here," Tlan said.

"But not from here. This was left untouched."

"Why, I wonder?" Tlan said.

They both paused, waiting for the answer from the ship, but none was forthcoming.

Yzal raised an eyebrow. "Now that is interesting. There must be some minerals that could have been mined here." At the words, the ship provided them with a breakdown of the gas giant's particles, demonstrating that there were minerals of considerable value.

Tlan frowned. "It's inexplicable that this would have been left."

Yzal nodded. "No reason not to take the time, especially once the Marauders were done. So why not?"

"I think we need to look at this another way. It was obviously left for a reason. But that reason has been hidden. Why?"

Yzal did not look at Tlan, ordering the ship to take them within the giant. The ship stayed in the outer regions of the planet, passing through clouds of ammonia, but nothing further was revealed.

"Was there a habitat nearby?" Yzal said. The ship answered in the negative.

Tlan raised a hand in question. "Do you have access to all files on the planet?" The ship answered in the affirmative. "Let us see them."

They spent an hour reading over what the ship showed them. Most of the files were taken from the archives the Marauders had stolen from the system's intelligences. It revealed little of interest. There had been a number of surveys of the planet's depths over the decades, one five years before the Marauders invaded, and there was exhaustive detail on every aspect of the planet's makeup.

Yzal was about to tell the ship to review the rest and conduct an analysis of what was there for possible connections to the message packets, when Tlan said, "Stop. Go back to that last image."

Dutifully the ship returned to the previous image, a three dimensional representation of certain convulsive cloud formations following a comet impact. One could see the point where various pieces of the comet had struck and the reverberations spreading out through the clouds. It was breathtaking and they both looked at it without speaking.

"I've seen this before," Tlan said at last, interrupting their reverie.

"Where?" Yzal said sharply, looking over at the other inspector.

"I'm not sure. Somewhere. Do an analysis of the Marauder fleet," Tlan said to the ship. "Is this found anywhere there?"

They received the answer a few short seconds later. The image was only available in the archives they were accessing at the moment.

"Would you have been looking at these files for some reason?" Yzal said, in a musing tone.

"No," Tlan said, staring hard at Yzal. Tlan's eyes widened slightly, for the barest fraction of a second, but Yzal noticed it.

"What is it?" Yzal said, on guard now.

"You. I saw it in your quarters. It wasn't this, not exactly, but it was..."

"A simulation..."

"With the lights on your wall," Tlan said, in wonder. "I almost didn't see it."

Both inspectors were silent, watching each other warily, waiting for one or the other to act. Neither moved, neither so much as breathed.

"What will you do?" Yzal said.

Tlan shrugged and put a hand, gentle and familiar on the other's shoulder. There were tears in Yzal's eyes and Tlan's as well. They looked about, as though conscious of someone watching them, but there was only the ship, silent as always. Without a word from either of them it set in a course for the portal, leaving the planet and the system behind.

JOURNEYS IN BETWEEN

THE RETURN

The hole was covered by a large and somewhat thick piece of styrofoam, like those used to protect electronics, that had gone yellow from the sun and was beginning to disintegrate. He had not come out for a very long time and, as such, was unaware of the state of its decay. The hole itself seemed to be somewhat decomposed, and—if it were possible—even smaller than when he had entered. But that was not surprising, for it had been so long since he had even strayed above to assure himself it was still intact.

It was when he saw that the last of his oranges had gone moldy that he grew fed up and decided to leave. How he had even lasted as long as he had was somewhat of a miracle. The days had been tedium upon tedium, with little to do but wait and nothing really to wait for. Long ago he had said there would be a sign, a signal, that would call him forth, but he had since forgotten what it was.

The moldy oranges—though they had begun to taste bitter long before—were sign enough, he determined. Time enough had been spent here, time enough indeed. The world beckoned him.

Shaking himself from immobility, and feeling the groan of his muscles and bones as they were forced into action, he crawled up the rickety ladder. It was slow, laborious going, his light from below soon vanishing as he ascended, leaving him in darkness. Each shake of the ladder as he moved up another rung sent a shower of dirt and leaves tumbling from above, hinting that perhaps all was not well there. The smell of fresh air still reached him though, and that suggested that something of the hole still

39

remained.

He was forced to brush a large number of thick spider webs away as he came nearer to the entrance, leaving him unsure as to why he had not been visited by the thousands of creatures the webs seemed to herald. Perhaps he had and he had simply forgotten. There were so many things that had drifted from his thoughts in the time he had spent below.

The smell of fresh air and damp earth seemed to grow stronger as he went, giving him a burst of energy that made him redouble his efforts on the ladder. He moved so quickly he nearly missed a step and had to cling tight to the ladder lest he tumble below. There would be no surviving that fall, he realized. He as no longer so young that he could trust his reflexes to save him.

At last he came to the pinnacle of his burrow and pushed the styrofoam aside, immediately blinding himself as the sunlight cascaded into the darkness. He leaned against the ladder, somewhat groggily for a time, his gnarled and coarse hands grasping its rough edges tightly, while his eyes gradually found their way in the world again. The first thing he distinguished was the house, a large and blurry form, and then the barren garden, from whose bowels he was emerging.

When he regained his eyesight he made his slow way out of the garden and down to the street corner. He was tired by then and had to sit on the sidewalk, with his feet resting on the pavement and his knees waving back and forth. His throat was very dry and he wondered where he might get some water. He was unsure where to look. It had been so long and the world was very different now. He did not even know who to ask or how.

That was when he was first noticed, with his head hangdog, staring at his ridiculous shoes. Most people took him in with a quick glance and a quizzical expression, perhaps a muttered question to a companion. Rumors began to spread and a local television crew arrived on the scene, looking bored and somewhat perturbed at the interruption to their schedule. They set up their camera and stood watching, waiting for the man to do something.

The camera crew's presence drew others who wanted to see what was happening. Most took a quick look and, seeing nothing of interest, moved on, but a few stayed, convinced that the man must soon do something. A lively discussion began amongst those gathered about the strangeness of it all. Many said this couldn't possibly be him, they had seen him at some time or another in a distant mausoleum, embalmed and on display.

"Why has he returned?" someone said at last.

There was a heavy silence following this question, until the woman who had spoken added, "I mean it must be for some reason, right?"

Murmurs of discussion followed, no one summoning the bravery needed to step forward and confront the man, who had now risen to his feet and taken a few unsteady steps. He turned, noticing at last the crowd assembled before him, and studied them with his unreadable eyes, a small grin—or perhaps it was a grimace?—marking his lips. That finished, he turned and made his way out beyond the city and into the desert.

FELIPE

Anna smiled as the security agent handed back her passport and moved forward to the conveyer belt. As she pulled out some trays from the stack and set her belongings in them, she glanced up and saw Felipe in the line across from her and frowned. They were racing each other, having chosen separate lines, and up until this point she had been ahead of him, her line moving at a steady pace.

She hurried with the trays, moving them onto the conveyer belt, and went to stand at the line in front of the x-ray machine.

"Shoes," the bored woman standing on the other side of the machine said.

Muttering under her breath, Anna quickly slid off her shoes and jammed them into the tray alongside her purse and jacket. Felipe, she saw, was still removing his belt. She had time. Back at the line, the woman waved her through and Anna went, savoring her triumph. It was short-lived, for the alarm sounded.

"Check your pockets, ma'am," the security guard said. "Keys. Cell phone. Jewelry."

Anna frantically searched her person for the stray item, but was unable to locate anything. "I'm sorry," she said. "There's nothing in my pockets."

"Come through again."

Anna did, and this time no alarm sounded. Still the woman insisted on waving her squeaking wand around Anna's body. Each change in pitch sounded ominous, but when she was done she waved Anna away. She went over to collect her things and met

Felipe, who was watching her grinning, beyond the security checkpoint.

"You owe me lunch," he said, as she came up to him.

"Damn machine. You did something, didn't you? Paid them off. Set up the machine to malfunction."

"My tentacles are everywhere," he said, with a smile.

They started walking toward their gate, crowds of people flowing around them.

"What's our gate," Felipe said, fumbling for his ticket.

"C44," Anna said. "It's always the farthest one."

"Never fails," Felipe said, scanning the signs ahead of them for directions. "We have lots of time though. If we see somewhere, we should stop to eat."

Anna nodded amiably and they continued on their way. They stopped at a burger place where the lineup seemed reasonable and ordered lunch, Anna's treat. They said little as they ate, both of them entertaining themselves by watching individuals among the crowd as it passed by. When they were finished they made their way to the gate. The flight was on time and they still had more than an hour until boarding, so they found seats and read, Felipe pulling out a book while Anna followed twitter on her phone.

A couple, with their young daughter, sat beside them as their boarding time approached. Her face was twisted into a foul expression, pushed there by her evident exhaustion. The couple looked haggard as well, obviously having spent the night on an airplane. Anna gave them a sympathetic smile. As she did, the girl began to wail uncontrollably.

"She didn't sleep at all, last night on the plane," her mother said, as the father collected the child in his arms and walked about the waiting area.

"Poor thing," Anna said.

When she turned back, she saw that Felipe was gone and smiled to herself. He had never had much patience for children, even less so for crying ones, so she was not surprised he had decided to absent himself. He'd left his book and backpack behind, so she assumed he had just gone to the bathroom, or for something to drink.

She turned her attention back to her phone, zoning out of all the noise, the squalling child, the constant hum of chatter, and the repeated airport announcements, glancing up from time to time to see if Felipe was returning. He did not, and she felt a flicker of annoyance that he had not told her where he was going, and mild concern that he was not back yet so close to their boarding time. Plenty of time yet, she reminded herself. It wasn't as though he could have gone far.

Ten minutes later, when the announcement came that they were ready to begin boarding, her concern turned to worry. She glanced over again to confirm that his things were still in the seat beside her. What could be taking him so long, she wondered, as people began to line up to board the plane. She checked her ticket and saw that they were seated in zone four, so there was still time for Felipe to return. Taking out her phone she texted him, asking where he was.

There was no response and he did not return in the next five minutes, as they boarded zones one through three and called for zone four. Feeling uneasy, but still not wanting to panic, she gathered her things and Felipe's and went to stand near the back of the line. She still expected Felipe to appear, a smile on his face, and a jest on his lips.

"You really didn't expect me to make it, did you?" he would say.

"I was fully prepared to leave you behind," she would reply and laugh, hiding the anxiety she was feeling.

She pulled out her phone again and called Felipe this time. The call went through to voicemail and the sound of his voice asking her to leave a message only added to her growing panic. Standing felt useless, so Anna decided to walk around the concourse in the hopes that she could spot Felipe. She wandered back toward the duty free shops, checking to see if he was inside browsing, and idled briefly by the washroom, considering asking one of the men going inside to look for her husband. That felt ridiculous though and she abandoned the thought, returning to the gate.

Zone five was boarding, and there were only a handful of people still waiting to get on the plane. Anna's hands were clammy with sweat and her mouth was dry. After texting and trying him on the phone again, she decided she had waited long enough and went to the gate desk and got the attention of one of the attendants who was not processing the passengers.

"This is so stupid," she said, "But my husband has wandered off and isn't answering his phone. I don't think he realizes the time.

Can you call him for boarding."

The woman smiled and said she would. A moment later Felipe's name was called out on the loudspeakers across the concourse. Surely he would come now, thought Anna. But he still did not appear.

There were no passengers left to board and the attendants came up to speak to her. "We're closing the door in five minutes, ma'am. If you don't board now, you'll miss your flight."

"I can't go without my husband," Anna said, her hands trembling.

They nodded sympathetically. "Unfortunately we can't wait. Federal regulations. We'll announce his name again"

"Of course," Anna said, trying and failing to smile.

She wandered away from the gate, fighting the urge to cry. The call for Felipe came again and she looked up, expecting to see him emerge from the crowd, harried and worried, but there. He did not and the world seemed to shrink around her, the light going dim. She could only see immediately around her, not to the far ends of the concourse and everyone's face was a blur. The air seemed strangled in her chest.

"Felipe," she called out, as loud as she could. "Felipe. Please."

She could feel people staring at her, but she ignored them, calling out again and again. In the distance, she could see three figures moving toward her, wearing official-looking uniforms.

THE EMISSARY

The leaves on the trees were all turning yellow and red as Jhern of Norne headed into the river valley. He took no pleasure in their gorgeous splendor, or the feeling of them beneath his feet, how they spun into the air as his boots struck them. The sound of the leaves meant anyone in the river would hear him coming—a dangerous enough proposition at home. Here in the Duke of Auzurn's territories, he might pay for it with his life. And their changing colors signaled the arrival of colder nights and stiff, miserable mornings, to say nothing of the fact that soon enough winter would be here.

It would be nearing winter by the time he arrived at his intended destination, assuming he made it there. Perhaps it would already have arrived, for he had heard that winter came early in Allemar, that fearsome place of bearded warriors. Before he reached that land, long before winter came, he first had to cross the Duke's territories and survive the Pass of Ghosts, which so few had managed to cross. And if he made it that far, there were the fiendish Skeletal Swamps, which it was said swallowed men whole and stole the souls of those who survived.

It was essential that Jhern do all this, risk life and limb for his Prince. The fate of his people, the fate of all Norne, depended upon it. The seas were rising and they would swallow their cities soon. Only the Allemar, with their magic, could spare them the terrible fate that awaited them.

And Jhern, emissary of his Prince, was the one entrusted to

bring that word. Along with his companions, but they were gone. Had all died so early upon this journey, to ensure that he would survive, that the message he carried, would be delivered. He had so far to go that it seemed impossible, but he knew he would have to. There was no other choice.

As he came to river's edge, he saw the narrow bridge ahead that the road he was on led to. He stood and looked it over cautiously, to see if there was any movement. This valley was home to woodcutters and the odd shepherd, but few others. The Auzurn authority barely extended here and Jhern did not expect to encounter any of the Duke's men. But one could never be too careful. There was too much at stake.

When he was satisfied that there was no one waiting for him, he started forward again, moving at a quick pace, not wanting to linger on the bridge or in the open for long. As he did, he was certain he saw a flash of movement across the river. It might have been a trick of light, but he thought not. He paused for an instant before continuing on, his hand straying to his belt to confirm that his sword and dagger were handy. He felt sure they would be necessary.

The bridge was a narrow, flimsy thing, strung across with rope and layered with boards. It swung slightly in the wind, the rope creaking in a way that made Jhern wonder how ancient it was. How many shepherds and woodcutters had made their way across it?

That was not his immediate concern though. More important was what awaited him on the other side.

He did not have to wait long to find out. Before he was even halfway across, a figure emerged from amidst the trees to block the way on the bridge's far end. It was a towering man, dressed in the Duke's colors, with a long broadsword at his side. Even from this distance, Jhern could see the ugly scar that ran from his eye down his cheek, disappearing beneath the armor. He paused for a moment to gather himself, drawing a deep breath.

Across from him the giant crossed his arms, a thin smile spreading on his face. "I know who you are little one. You are the Emissary of Norne."

Jhern almost stumbled, such was his surprise. How could this Auzurn know who he was? "What of it?" he cried out.

An evil smile formed on the giant's face. "Your journey ends here. You shall not pass."

Jhern stopped where he was, very conscious of the swaying of the bridge and the groaning of the ropes. He was, he judged, a little more than halfway across, making retreat all but impossible. A swing of the giant's sword would sever the ropes and send him tumbling into the torrent below.

As if to confirm this, the giant said. "You must come here and face me. If you turn aside I will send you into the river below."

"Why not do that now?" Jhern said, in frustration. One look at the giant and his massive arms told him he had little hope of defeating the man in hand to hand combat.

"I will give you a fair fight, as is honorable. It is more than the Norne ever gave my father and mother when they set upon my village."

Jhern resisted a bitter laugh. Of course the fate of the Norne would be decided by some peasant villager who had been wronged years ago, probably by men who had long since passed to the other side of the Veil. And if Jhern failed here, the rest of his people would join them soon enough. He had to find a way.

"You call me emissary. Do you understand what is at stake? The fate of all Norne. We will fall under the sea in a span of years, unless the Allemar help us. And that is no sure thing."

As Jhern spoke, he glanced down at the coursing river, trying to ascertain whether he could survive the fall and the current. It was unlikely. He was a poor swimmer and the water was fast and wide.

"I know what you journey for," the giant said. "I have been following you these last weeks. I have been waiting for just such a moment as this."

"You know what I journey for and yet you would condemn us all to the fate of your parents. The men who wronged you, wronged you. There are thousands of children who you would condemn to death. They are innocent."

"They are born of Norne," the giant said. "In my eyes they are as guilty as you. Vengeance shall be mine. Come across now. There is no escape for you. Face this like a man and perhaps you will see your people saved."

The giant gestured and Jhern gave a small, helpless shrug and started forward. As he walked across, he tried to think of some strategy to defeat the giant. None came to mind, except to wound him in the leg somehow and run for his life. Even that might lie beyond his capabilities.

He was a step or two from the bridge's end when the board he stepped on gave way, sending him plunging toward the river. Flailing desperately he managed to get one hand upon the next board and he clung to it by his fingertips. His free hand sought the board and found purchase, but he still had to pull himself up, back onto the bridge.

Seeing him fall, he giant cried out in fear and rage and rushed onto the bridge, a hand extended. But his weight upon the bridge jarred it and set it swinging, shaking Jhern's grip. One hand and then the other fell away. The giant reached him too late, Jhern felt their fingertips brush together before he fell into the water.

The last thing he heard was the giant's bitter roar at his revenge denied, before the river carried him away, pulling him under.

GIRL LEADING A BLIND MINOTAUR
THROUGH THE NIGHT

The girl had yet to speak. The bird that fluttered from shoulder to shoulder gave voice for both of them. It had announced, upon their entering the hovel where the Minotaur had spent the last days of his journey, that he was to come with them. The Minotaur had stood up and allowed his hand to be taken by the girl. There seemed no point in asking questions or demanding explanations. He was at the mercy of this girl and her bird, until they reached the end of their portion of his journey.

Such had been his fate for these last months, since he had begun this ordeal, broken and fleeing into the night. He had been forced to endure much and had to learn to trust in those he did not know and could not see. Would they betray him to those who were looking for him? He would not know until it was too late.

The fact it was a girl, hardly more than ten years old to judge by the size of her hand and his sense of her height—he was becoming quite adept at judging a person's size by the feel of their movement—was somewhat reassuring. Though he knew it should not be. Girls, whatever their age, could be bought. Everyone had a price, as he knew too well.

In spite of all he had lost, in spite of the meanness of this existence—going from one safe house to another, never having a home, indebted to strangers he could never repay—he never thought of stopping or slipping into despair. There was no use for self-pity. This was what fate had chosen for him, and he would continue to wander for as long as fate allowed. He expected it would not be long.

"How much farther?" he asked, when he could stand the silence no longer.

The girl shrugged and the bird said, "It will take us the evening to get to the river."

What river they were heading for, and what happened once they reached it, was left unstated. Most likely, the girl and the bird did not know. How many others had they conducted along this trail in the dead of the night?

After some time the bird spoke again. "You needn't worry. We meet our bargains."

The Minotaur did not reply. Words mattered little, as they all knew. It was actions that counted.

They walked the rest of the night, stopping only once to rest, and then only briefly. To the Minotaur's relief, the trail they were on was well-trodden and the terrain it wandered over was relatively gentle. With his sight taken from him, to say nothing of the other grievous injuries he had suffered, such small mercies were welcome.

The limp in his right leg, a result of a broken hip that had healed improperly, grew more pronounced as the morning approached. It was always this way and he offered no complaint. The bird and girl would not care to hear it. It was an injury from another lifetime, a life taken from him, a constant reminder of that loss. Only in his exhaustion did the memories, that he kept so carefully at bay, return. He was helpless to stop them.

Morning was nearing when they halted again. The Minotaur could sense dawn's arrival by the change in the air around him. The bird cooed softly into the darkness, a song that the Minotaur was certain was not his. After a time, someone whistled in response, some distance away, and girl began to lead the Minotaur forward.

He stiffened, he could not help himself. Here was potential for danger. The girl and the bird had not betrayed him yet, but if they were planning to, now would be when he found out. Someday it would happen, it was inevitable, he could only hope he would be spared one more night.

The trail led down into the river valley, leaves brushing against his face and shoulders as they went. The ground was uneven and he had some difficulty keeping his feet under him and had to lean on the girl. She took his weight without issue, surprising him. As they descended, the sound of the river came to him, a hushed murmur that gradually became louder.

They halted again and the Minotaur could hear the bird fly from the girl's shoulder. He could hear it whisper a greeting and receive one in return. The man who replied had a strangled voice, that sounded to the Minotaur as though it could not rise much above a whisper. He was very near.

"This is your passage," the bird said, loud enough for the Minotaur to hear.

The man grunted and the girl's small hand was replaced by his hard, callused one. The Minotaur was led into the river, the water cold on his ankles, and the man helped him into the front of a small boat. The man pushed the vessel off from the shore, grunting under his breath, before climbing in behind the Minotaur.

The Minotaur did not speak and the man seemed disinclined to as well, busy working at the paddles, dragging the boat across the current. The night that was left to them seemed still and silent, only the water beneath them disturbing the peace. The Minotaur listened to it, letting the sound lull him, as the boat went to the river's far side, taking him to what awaited him there.

ON DOWN THE ROAD

"Thanks for coming Cliff," Walter said as they both climbed into the pickup, the dog nestling at Cliff's feet.

Cliff nodded, but did not reply. The day was hot and the truck, which had been sitting out in the sun, was hotter and his back was already damp with sweat. He rolled down the window and rested his arm gingerly against the scalding hot metal. The dog looked up grinning at him, in spite of the uncomfortable position it had contorted itself into.

Walter rolled down his own window and started the truck, humming to himself as he did. The radio, as always was tuned to 770, the talk radio station from Edmonton. In afternoon's, which it was now, Rutherford was on. Cliff found him insufferable. Walter did too, but he enjoyed listening to him. Enjoyed disagreeing and getting annoyed and laughing at how wrong he was.

Walter headed out to the road and turned north, the dust from the gravel leaving a broad wake behind them. It had been a dry year, the pastures were already more brown than green, and the green of the fields was fast turning to yellow. Harvest would be only a couple of weeks away, or sooner, if the warm weather held. It would be a poor one as well—there had been little rain that spring and none in the summer. Walter said it was as bad as he had seen it, as bad as when he was a kid in the thirties.

"I just don't feel comfortable heading up to the pastures by myself anymore," Walter said, as if the silence of the last minutes had not happened. "Not as young as I used to be. Of course, before I would've taken Jane."

Cliff opened his mouth but did not reply. He didn't know quite what to say, didn't have the words. Jane had been Walter's wife for over fifty five years. She had died the summer before, a summer as hot and dry as this one.

Cliff didn't have to say anything though. Walter kept talking, as he drove down the road at an ambling pace.

"That calf is probably dead, but we have to go see if we can find it. Might've just gotten separated from its mother. I remember we had a heifer, got her head stuck between the branches of a tree and couldn't figure out how to get out. Almost died before we found her."

Cliff nodded. He had heard the story before, as he had heard so many of his grandfather's stories. In spite of the open windows on the truck, it still felt stultifying. Or perhaps it was just the same old conversations, the same old trips down the same old roads. That fall he would be off to university. He was counting the days until he would be free of this tedium. Life felt as though it were happening somewhere else, while he chased after presumably dead calves in pastures somewhere off in the middle of nowhere.

It was a half hour drive up to the pasture. Once there they made their interminable away across its three sections, scouting for the lost calf. Walter insisted on heading to every low-lying spot where a few trees had sprouted up. The cattle would often gather in them during the heat of the summer, or in the spring when their might still be water lying in them. Now all them were empty, the cattle clustered near the center of the pasture where a slough and a dugout provided their water.

When they had gone through the copses of trees on the south side of the pasture, they proceeded through the herd to check and see if the missing calf had reappeared. Walter concentrated on the various calves, while Cliff stared off at the vast horizon and the cloudless sky, listening to the buzzing insects and chirping birds.

"I don't see him," Walter said when the truck had made its way through the last of the herd.

"Me either," Cliff said, straight faced.

Walter turned the truck north and they went through the rest of the pasture. There was no sign anywhere of the missing calf, not even any bones whitening in the sun. "It might have gotten out through the fence somewhere and not been able to get back,"

Walter mused.

Cliff nodded, though he wasn't really listening anymore, his mind already on what he could do once they got home. The calf was gone and there didn't seem any point belaboring the issue. It wasn't as though they could solve the mystery of its disappearance, unless its body showed up somewhere.

"Maybe it ended up in with MacTierney's cattle," Walter continued, oblivious of Cliff's sudden restlessness. "They'll let us know if they see him though."

As they drove out of the pasture, they passed by an oil well that had recently been capped. Walter stopped the truck to look over the fence the workers had put up around the well, making sure it was in good shape. "Now," Walter said, with a shake of his head. "What do you suppose the chances are one of those boys had a rifle and decided to get himself some steak while he was up here?"

Cliff shrugged. "Maybe."

"Maybe," Walter said, nodding. "Maybe."

They returned home, Walter whistling to himself and Cliff watching the dust pooling behind them in the side mirror. Neither of them spoke until they were almost back to the yard.

"So you're off to school next month," Walter said.

"Yeah," Cliff said.

"Getting excited? Got everything ready?"

"I guess so," Cliff said, answering both questions or neither.

"Well, I hope you enjoy it. It's good to get out and see the world while you can," Walter said, looking across the cab of the truck at his grandson.

They were within sight of the farm by then. On the one side of the road was the yard, with Walter's house and Cliff's home, where he lived with his parents. On the other side was the house Walter had grown up in, where his parents had first settled. It was dilapidated, windows broken and paint peeling, leaning slightly to the side, and looking as though a stiff wind might send it toppling.

Walter nodded at the place, his expression thoughtful. "I didn't go very far in life," he said. "Just across the road."

A NEW CAREER IN A NEW TOWN

The dead ruled the back roads. They had worn and weathered faces, eyes hard against the horizon. They were staring at that unwavering point, always visible, no matter which direction one was traveling. The horizon beyond the horizon and the sky beyond the sky. No matter where one looked, it was there, and the dead were always walking toward it, though they could never arrive at that destination. It was the land of the living, and they had passed beyond it.

Xue had as well, though he was not dead. Not yet, anyway. He avoided the dead, hiding himself along the roadside whenever he saw them approaching. Caution was his watchword in this place, for he had none of the powers of the inhabitants here. He was a mere swordsman, practitioner of those sacred arts, though no master. His failures were that of any man, and for them he had been punished—cursed—and now he found himself wandering this land, just as the dead did, hoping somehow to reach that point on the horizon and cross to the world beyond.

Xue stayed to the nether regions and the back roads, for beyond them were things far worse than the dead. If he wanted to return to the land of living he needed to stay alive, a difficult proposition in this realm, where ghouls, demons, and things not even imagined by mortals existed. Had he understood the terrible cost his actions would carry, the damnation he would incur for his wrongs, he would not have been so quick to act.

"Vengeance is a luxury only the rich can afford," his master had once told him. He had been correct, but Xue had not been willing to listen. Now he rued his impatience and anger every day.

The road upon which he walked during this endless day—for evening never came here, just as morning never returned anew—was a trail worn by an unending multitude of walkers. Dust stirred with his every step. He was on a vast and arid plain, that seemed to cross all of the realm here, the sky above vast and incomprehensible. It was blue, though somewhat faded and drawn, with specks of clouds adrift within. They never seemed to move and the weather never changed. It was as though the sky was caught in an instant forever. And he was ensnared in it as well.

It had been hours since he had stopped walking, or encountered anyone, and so he stepped off the road when he spied a copse of trees nearby that hinted at a spring. He headed toward it, thinking to rest for a spell, more for a change than out of any need. He did not sleep here or even tire. But that was not something he had become used to as yet. Often, he would lie down in some secluded place out of sight of the road and close his eyes, feigning to sleep. His mind would go as still as the sky above him, but never once did he slip from consciousness. He could not. This place was a kind of dreaming.

The copse of twisted and gnarled trees, branches heavy with ugly leaves, more black than green, held a spring as he had guessed. The water he found there was fetid and stinking, a sickly color that reminded him of what was found in the intestines of an animal being slaughtered. Though it was repulsive to look upon and smell, he sat down beside it, putting his back against a tree. He closed his eyes and listened to the wind hissing through the trees. It sounded odd and a moment later he realized why. None of the branches were moving.

Soon they were. Xue's eyes flashed open and he saw a girl standing over him, a dagger clenched between her teeth. He blinked, wondering how she had managed to get so near without his realizing. She had the drawn and haggard look all the dead had, in spite of her evident youth.

"What are you going to do?" he asked her, judging how near his hand was to his sword and how close she was to him.

She seemed taken aback by his question and froze for just a moment. Xue used that time to draw his own dagger from his belt and press it against her throat. Her eyes went very wide.

"Do the dead care about dying in this place?" he said.

"I'm not dead," she said, spitting her blade to the ground and raising her hands in surrender. "I'm just here."

Xue picked up her dagger with his free hand, never taking his eyes from her and not letting his blade slip from her throat. The dead were not to be trusted, not even one so young as this. This was their realm and it was a place of the damned.

"I imagine that's what all the dead say. They all think they can cross back to the world. I can see it in the way they stare."

The girl gave him a quizzical look. "You don't want to go back?"

"More than anything," Xue said. "But I actually can. I am here because of what I did, not because I died. I was cursed. Damned for eternity."

The girl shrugged. "We all were. Why else would we be in this place?"

Xue nodded for the girl to sit down across from him. She did, moving cautiously, her eyes always upon him, careful to keep herself just beyond his arm's reach. Xue kept his dagger ready in his hand and adjusted himself so that he would be ready to respond to any attack.

"How long have you been here?"

The girl shrugged again. "I don't know. Time is not the same here. The days have no end."

"No they do not," Xue said. "I myself have only recently arrived."

"It doesn't matter," the girl said, stealing a glance off to the fetid pool.

"What do you mean?" Xue said, not taking his eyes from her.

"You think because you came here recently that it will be easier for you to return. But time is different here. It doesn't work that way at all."

"What do you know of these things girl?"

"Girl," she scoffed. "I'm not so young as I look."

Xue was about to contest her statement, but studying her more closely he saw that she was not so young as he had at first believed. Her sleight stature confused the matter, as did the drawn skin on her face.

"So now what?" she said, studying him carefully. "Are you going to kill me?"

"What would be the point? You're already dead," he said, standing up.

He looked past her into the trees, thinking he had heard the trees rustling again. When he turned back to her she was gone, as was her dagger, which he had slipped in his belt. He whirled around, expecting her to be there with her dagger ready to plunge into his back. She was not there either. It was only when she whistled that he caught sight of her standing across the fetid spring.

"Space is not the same here either," she said.

"So I see," Xue said.

"You have a lot to learn, if you intend to return to the living."

She put her dagger away in her belt, a gesture of peace. Xue followed suit, though he knew not to trust her entirely. She had come to him with a dagger in her teeth, with the obvious intention of doing him harm.

"And you propose a partnership I suppose."

"Why not? These roads are dangerous. And to get to where we're going, we'll need to go to places far more dangerous."

"Where are we going?" he said, his hands still tense at his side, ready to draw his swords.

She pointed to the spot of the horizon they both could see.

"You're dead," he said.

"None of us here is alive. Not in any way that matters."

He considered what she said, realizing that she was right. About everything. "Where to first?"

"There is a town up ahead. We start there."

Xue nodded and followed her from the swamp back to the road.

SECURITY

"Goddammit," Ali said, biting her lip as she looked at the screen above the counter at her gate.

There was no departure time listed. Nor was there any indication of a delay. She looked out at the bridge that connected the terminal to the plane, but there was none attached. And there was no one at the counter. She wandered back to look a the departures screen down the corridor to confirm that she was at the correct gate.

There it was: Vancouver to Winnipeg, Gate A31. The screen said the departure was on-time, though no actual time was listed, which Ali thought odd.

She went back to the gate, hoping to find an agent, but there was still no one at the counter. There was a man standing there, staring ahead and Ali approached him. "Sorry," she said, "are you on the flight to Winnipeg."

He nodded. "Yeah. They say it's here, but there's no plane. And there's no one here."

"There hasn't been anyone at the counter, then?"

He shook his head. "No. Computers aren't even turned on." He gestured to the monitors on the counter, which Ali saw were black.

"This is so weird."

"So strange," he said. "There's a lot of people here though. Can't all be wrong, right?"

"I guess," Ali said. She wasn't so sure. These were airlines after all. They would cancel a flight without telling anyone. Or move it to another terminal and sell all the seats to people on standby, not bothering to refund all those who were stuck here unawares.

She told herself to be patient, there was plenty of time until her flight, and went to find a seat in the waiting area. It was difficult, with dozens and dozens of frustrated looking people sitting and staring at the empty counter. Ali found it comforting in some strange way. They could all be miserable together.

As time went on the waiting area filled up. Nearly every seat was filled and the open area around the gate counter was nearly impassable, with hordes of people staring at phones or the tarmac where a plane had yet to appear. Anyone who looked vaguely official was immediately confronted by ten or more people demanding answers. None were forthcoming. Ali could hear at least five different conversations with various agents, trying to placate the irate people who were waiting for a flight that had not materialized.

At a certain point, it dawned on her that there were far more people gathered here than could possibly fit on the plane. She could see others reaching the same awareness. Something was very odd about all this. How could so many people end up at this airport gate, awaiting a flight that no one at the airline seemed to know anything about, except that it was supposed to be taking off?

They were half an hour past their scheduled departure time, the restlessness of the crowd beginning to sound dangerous, when the some official-looking people appeared and began to move through the crowd. Ali saw them asking questions, with that blank face that all people in authority used when they were trying not to betray what they knew was going on.

By the time they arrived to question her, Ali had had enough. "Can someone explain what the hell is going on here?"

"We were hoping you could," the woman in the pantsuit said, sounding infuriatingly calm.

"What do you think I'm doing? I'm trying to catch my plane. I've been here for over an hour and no one seems to know what's going on."

The woman glanced at her partner. "When did you book this flight?"

"I..." Ali started to answer, but could not find the words. She could not recall.

"And where are you going?"

"Winnipeg," she said immediately, though doubt began to creep in as soon as she spoke.

"Do you know anyone in Winnipeg?"

Ali hesitated. "No."

"Any business that would take you there?"

"No." Ali shuddered, as a terrible awareness began to take hold.

As she struggled to find an answer to any of the questions she had been asked, the female officer answered a phone call. "Yes. Everyone here. The same as before. We're bringing them all in as soon as the wagons show up."

The officers left Ali without saying another word. Ten minutes later she, and everyone else, was escorted out of the terminal into large vans by agents, in uniforms she did not recognize. Everyone in her van was mystified as to what was happening and a few were furious. "If I've done something wrong, arrest me. There's no reason for this," one man said.

"I don't think these are police," Ali said.

"Then what the hell is going on?"

No one had an answer. None was forthcoming once they arrived at their destination, a huge warehouse surrounded by a tall gate. Ali caught a brief glimpse of the river beyond the compound as she was led, along with the others, into the warehouse. The agents organized everyone into groups by some method Ali could not discern. She, and about thirty others, were taken into a windowless room near the entrance and ordered to form a line. One by one they were called up and taken into yet another room.

When Ali reached the front of the line, she asked the agent directing people what was happening. "Just processing," he said, as he motioned her forward.

She went into the next room and was made to empty her purse and open her bags, all of which were searched thoroughly. When that was done she went through a metal detector, followed by a careful search by a woman. Nothing was revealed by these searches, at least nothing the agents found interesting, and Ali was told to go into the next room.

There she found all the other groups of passengers slowly gathering as they too went through processing. The room they were in was massive, with ceilings that reached to the top of the warehouse, and enough space to hold three or four times that many people. Ali looked around but, much to her annoyance, she couldn't find anyone who might be able to answer any of her questions. After a few minutes aimless wandering she gave up and joined the others who had found a place on the floor to sit.

They waited for an hour, with no sign of any agents and no explanation of how long they might be expected to remain there. More and more people continued to arrive as time went on. Far more, Ali realized with a growing horror, than she had come with from the airport. She got up again, feeling panicked, and went to one of the doors where people were coming in from being processed, marching up to one of the agents.

"What's going on? How long am I supposed to just sit here and wait?"

The agent did not even glance in her direction. "Ma'am, I'm going to have to ask you to get to the back of the line for processing."

"I've already been through processing. I want to talk to someone who can tell me what's going on." Ali could hear her voice and it sounded hysterical. People were looking up from the line, which stretched out the next door, with some mild curiosity.

"Ma'am, I understand. But you've come out of the containment area and now you need to be processed again. Please move to the back of the line."

Ali stared at him for a moment, feeling fury and desperation in equal measure. What if I don't, what if I just stay here, she wanted to say. The agent was not even looking at her, already going over the next person's luggage. Ali sighed and started back to try to find the end of line.

VOYAGE'S END

A ship, alight upon the sea, surging upon the waves as it's crew stands watch, eyes straining forward, alert to the horizon. This was the image that came to her mind as Ance whiled away the interminable hours in this desolate place. A ship coming to take her home.

She had long ago stopped counting the days, it had grown too depressing by far. No matter how many she marked off her calendar or in her diaries, the remainder still loomed ahead, the weight of them the same, as backbreaking as the work of the porters who carry her belongings up and down the mountains of this cruel and barbaric place. Her greatest fear was that her husband would arrive at one of their homes, on one of his occasional acknowledgments that they were in fact married, to announce that the Viceroy had extended his term and they would be remaining for another five years.

It was a thought beyond bearing. Every day she was surrounded by hundreds of people, most of whom could not speak more than a civilized word or two to her. Their disdain was evident in every gesture they made, in every expression when they thought she was not paying attention. They were doing things to her food as well, she was certain. She always felt weak and ill, though perhaps that was just the abominable climate, so frigid and damp.

One day, as she spent another afternoon lost in pointless reverie, it came to her that it did no good to idly dream of such things, she needed to make chance bend to her will and act. Her husband spent most of his days pretending she did not exist, it could be easily done. She called her porters and had them gather her belongings and set off from her home in the misty highlands.

Ance told no one the purpose of her journey, swearing the porters to secrecy under threat of banishment. Would her husband even notice her absence? It was galling to her that he had insisted she come to this land, to exile herself from all she knew. His chances of advancement in the colonial hierarchy were better if he were seen to be a family man, he had told her, and she had seen the logic of it. And after all, they were husband and wife, and she had longed for his touch.

Her destination was the nearest harbor, a day's journey away. She was unfamiliar with it, but she felt she could not risk the three day journey to the one she had disembarked from. Three days was enough time for her husband to catch up to her once he discerned her intentions, as he surely would. He was no fool after all, he had played her for one.

It was only after he had welcomed her to her new home in the highlands that she came to understand the true nature of the situation and why he had been so desperate for Ance to join him. It was not love or longing that had driven him to beckon her. He had taken up with one of the local women. She traveled with him as he surveyed all the territories he governed and they had spawned several half-witted children. What talk there would have been in the capital with his goings on, which he had foolishly hoped to quiet with his wife's arrival. It had not, for he had refused to so much as hide his relationship with the other woman, carrying on as ever, with the result that his position in the hierarchy had not improved and Ance had suffered shame and embarrassment that she had been so duped by this rogue.

Their precarious journey down from the highlands passed without incident and Ance felt certain of her chances for success as they arrived at the harbor. But as the emerald blue of the ocean came glistening into sight, she saw that she had deluded herself. There was only a little fishing village at the far end of the narrow bay. The water was speckled with the canoes of the men out fishing for the day, but no vessel of any size would come here.

She wanted to throw herself to the ground and weep at the wretchedness of it all, to curse the porters for deceiving her. But she had only herself to blame. She had let herself become deceived by a reverie. Bad enough to be led on by a rogue as she had by her husband, now Ance had deluded herself. Madness was surely only a step away.

Just as she as about to tell the porters to return her and her belongings to the highlands and return to her fate, a ship appeared around the bend of the bay, curving along the coastline toward the harbor. Ance watched dumbstruck as the vessel dropped anchor and a small boat was sent ashore. Before any of the porters had time to react she ran toward the incoming boat, wading into the water and crying out for help.

"Please, please," she said. "These men have kidnapped me. Take me on your ship, my family will gladly pay you a reward for my safe return."

The men on the boat, faces heavy with tangled beards, squinted past her at the porters who remained on the beach watching what was happening. At a nod from the man at the head of boat, two others pulled her aboard while the rest loaded their muskets and let fire at the servants. She saw one porter fall on the beach while the rest began to run back up the beach, before she turned her head away, unable to watch.

The boat turned around and made its way back to the vessel, as she babbled her incoherent thanks to her saviors. None of them replied, their eyes intent on the beach to see if there would be any response to their shots. The boat was raised up back onto the vessel and she was brought before the captain, a scarred and vicious looking man who studied her through narrow eyes as she begged him again to return her home, telling him a tale of kidnapping and sorrow.

As she finished he nodded and said, in an unfamiliar accent, "Aye, we'll see you brought home."

She was so overwhelmed she could not find the words to speak and she worried she would collapse in a faint. The captain uttered a command in a dialect she did not understand and the vessel began to turn about. She looked about surreptitiously at her new companions and saw they were all gaunt faced and hollow-eyed, dressed in tatters and with a hunger to their expression that gave her chills.

THINGS THAT YOU DREAM

There are lights. Flashing upward through the darkness, arcing toward some unknown destination. You reach out for them instinctively, though you know they are far from you and from an age long ago lost to memory. No records survive, only tales, most of which you know are half truths and utter lies, told to placate you or to make the teller seem a warlock or adjutant. No one you know can claim such a storied lineage. Those who can left long before, abandoning you to this place.

You imagine what the lights are, fevered dreams, all yearning. They are immortality. That much you know, though you cannot put it into words just how that might be. They are a world gone, a world of forever. The warlocks riding their dragons through nights without end, weaving their spells. Those places died long ago and the roads to reach them have been destroyed.

The world is getting colder. The skies forever overcast and grim, but bearing no moisture. Day by day by day it seems the passage forward grows narrower and narrower as the fire at the heart of all things grows dim. When you close your eyes at night, huddling closer to whoever is near, you dream of the inner workings, those gears and tubes and mechanisms that have kept turning for all these lifetimes. Time without measure. But now their time is growing short, each turn of the gear growing slower and slower.

You know the answer lies within those fearsome mechanisms,

which only the warlocks and their acolytes knew the inner workings of. In your dream you walk among them and there the secrets of the warlocks are revealed to you. When you awake you know that you will go.

There are mirrors and pulsing lights at the heart of all things. It is beyond comprehension, beyond imagining. Is it dangerous to stand here, to look on in awe? You cannot know. You go ever forward, in search of what you don't know. Something, some sign or invention, that makes the mechanisms that whir in your head spark with realization. But nothing comes. These are things for warlocks and acolytes, those who can animate matter into being. There is no place for you here.

And so you wander through corridors and rooms, up and down stairs, twisting and winding your way to where you don't know. Has anyone ever stood in the places you have stood? Not in memory. There was no reason, and now that there is, it is far too late. Those who knew these ways are gone. Those whose hands could make pinpricks of light dance have vanished and left us bereft.

Finally you run out of passages to traverse and come to a portal sealed tight with arcane runes scripted upon it. It is bespelled by the warlocks, but those spells have grown weak and a word and a twist of its wheel sets it open. From there you step into a new and impossible world.

There is void and nothingness everywhere. Far into the distance are stars beyond number. You drift into the ether, The universe is beneath you, suddenly seeming miniscule, no more than a speck in a greater whole. In a moment it is gone and you are left utterly alone, galaxies unfurling in the dusk of your pupils.

MONSTERS AND MEN

THE INVADER

There were no objects distant and unrecognizable on the horizon, no people who spoke, in voices tinged with madness, of having been kidnapped by unseen creatures, no armada of stars filling the night skies above. One day they were not there and the next they were, with no sign of how they had done so. There was no panic, no riots in the streets, or calls to arms, for it was obvious to all there would be no point to it. They were among them, walking the streets and going about their business as if they had always been there.

No one even thought it particularly strange, though on some distant level, deep within their consciousness, they knew it was. They were aliens and they had seized the planet without so much as a word of defiance. How had it happened? Something must have occurred. Something terrible and awful, to make them surrender so completely. But no one seemed to know. This was the way it had always been, they said, even as they knew it was not so.

It was difficult to describe the invaders. They were not human and they were...something. Words failed them, as did their memories. The shape and substance of the aliens seemed to dissipate as soon as their minds tried to focus on them. It was as though they were figments of dreams, and yet there could be no doubt they were there. Their presence was palpable everywhere one went. It left them with nothing to fight, nothing to even focus their anxiety on.

Strangest of all was how little things changed. The invaders were among them, shadowing their thoughts, filling their every step with doubt, and yet they did little concrete. Businesses still opened and closed, people went to work and ran their errands, and returned home to their families. But all the while the aliens were there, not observing, not disrupting, simply there, as if they had always been and always would be.

Things went on like this for some time, and people began to wonder if this was simply how existence would be from now an. An oppressiveness hung over all their thoughts, from which they could not escape. The invaders did not appear to notice the growing melancholy of the planet. They continued about their days as though there was nothing untoward or sinister about the aliens' presence at all. It only added to the growing hysteria people could feel clawing at the edges of their thoughts.

What were the aliens doing? Nothing in particular it seemed, living lives that seemed not to intersect with anyone. No one saw them returning to their homes, or sleeping, or eating. They were simply present. That absence of purpose began to seem more and more ominous, for they clearly had the power and ability to do so much more. They had taken control of the planet without struggle and kept the entire populace in a state of unease, unable to so much as explain why they felt as they did.

Nothing stays as it is, entropy demands it, and the universe gradually unspools. One day a woman named Anj awoke to find one of the invaders in her home looking upon her expectantly. She wanted to scream, but could not find the will to speak. The alien did not say anything either, it simply watched as she got up and prepared for the day. Anj showered and dressed and put on her makeup, palpably aware of the invader's presence, yet unable to stop her compulsion to go about her morning as though it were any other.

Normally she did not make breakfast at home, preferring to eat at the office after she had settled in with some coffee and checked her emails. Today was different. Today she decided to take the time to cook eggs, and not just any eggs, perfectly rounded soft poached eggs. She set a pot with water and a bit vinegar on the stove to boil. Turning from that she made coffee and set some bread in the toaster.

It was all very odd, because she needed to be going soon or she would be late for work. She was unconcerned though. She could find some explanation, or call in sick and not show up at all. What about tomorrow? She understood now that she would not be going to work tomorrow either, or the next day, and she began to feel anxious about that as the water started to boil. She cracked the eggs into custard cups and began to stir the boiling water as she poured the eggs in.

There was a knock at the door and she went to answer it. Her neighbor Zee was standing there, blurry eyed. Anj stepped aside and allowed her in, neither of them speaking. She returned to the eggs, not watching as Zee began to dance the nae nae in front of the invader. It was all so much like a dream, the thought came to Anj, but it was not a dream. She could feel the cloud of humidity from the boiling water striking her face, could hear each step Zee took, all while the invader watched them both, there and not there.

How to explain it? She could not. She put the bread down in the toaster. When it was done the eggs were as well and she retrieved them from the water, nestling them on the bread. The plate ready, she set it on the table with cutlery alongside. Zee was sounding short of breath from her dancing but she continued without ceasing and Anj went to join her as the invader sat down to eat.

AURORA

Dorvel watched from the station's observation deck as the beast leapt from the inner ring surrounding the gas giant. It appeared to float momentarily, suspended in the vacuum of space, before it plunged back into the ring, disappearing from sight. She turned her attention back to the monitors tracking its progress, knowing it would be several minutes before it appeared again. The rings were constituted almost entirely of frozen water, formed into intricate crystalline structures, and the beast was drinking.

Dorvel was observing it, and had been for almost the entirety of the last two days, because it was pregnant, extremely so, and her superiors expected the calf to be born any day now. Birthing was a delicate process for any animal, all the more so for one that spent its days in the space, as the scow did. This being the distinctly unimaginative name given the creatures by the Councilmen who first encountered them. The name—that some found amusing, but which Dorvel had long grown tired of—being a play on the ancient meaning of the word, a type of old earth sea-going vessel and an abbreviation of the words 'space cow'.

The scow surfaced again, this time very near the station, and Dorvel's breath was taken away. Their vastness still had the power to startle, even for someone who had spent so much of her life working with the creatures. This time the beast did not return within the ring, having drunk its fill, letting the gravity of the planet pull her into orbit. Dorvel checked the time and made a quick calculation of how much water she had drank, assuring herself that the scow and its progeny were well fed.

Everything now was of critical importance. Nothing could be left to chance, she well knew. This was the third scow she had shepherded to birth in her ten years as Head Veterinarian for the Council. None of the other calves had survived more than a day or two. It had been a lifetime since anyone had even seen a calf or a youngling scow, even as the number of adult scows dwindled year by year, their stock ravaged by the hardships of space and the Councils seemingly endless wars.

There were many theories as to the origins of the scows, none definitive. How had something evolved that was ideal for deep space journeys, able to traverse the emptiness of space with minimal sustenance? How serendipitous was it that such a creature should exist with its intricate and cavernous interior chambers that could be easily fitted with life support systems and other necessities for humans to inhabit them? It was something tailor made for transporting material and people across the vast expanses of the universe. Many scientists had reached the conclusion, one shared by the Head Veterinarian, that some other, long lost and forgotten being, had created the scows for its since vanished empires.

The Councilmen who first came across the scow herd and managed to explore the creatures' interiors, noting the beasts' apparent indifference to their presence, had reached much the same conclusion and had set about taming them. It was a monumental task, and not without its losses, but the Councilmen persevered and triumphed. Guidance sensors and other tech was soon added to the scows nervous system so that they could be directed by anyone, though generally it was left to the Teamsters Guild that arose from those early attempt to break the scows.

The Veterinarian Guild, of which Dorval was a proud member, came into existence around the same time, and now the use and care of the scows was almost entirely routine, as routine as anything in space could be, with only the pregnancy and birth of the creatures proving persistently difficult. Which is what had brought Dorvel to this lonely edge of space, near this gas giant, utterly devoid of life, to worry and fret and stand by helplessly as Aurora gave birth.

There were those who said one shouldn't name the scows. They were not individuals, not in the way humans were. Did they even care for their young? Presumably, though few had witnessed such interactions and records were scarce. This then, assuming all went to plan—and oh what a fearful assumption to make—would be the singular triumph of Dorvel's career. There was nowhere else in the universe she desired to be than here with Aurora, a name she had given the creature, at least in her own thoughts. She had even whispered it aloud within the scow when she was certain she was alone.

"Anything?" Galesh, Aurora's Teamster, said as he entered the observation deck.

"No change," she said, not looking away from the observation window. Though neither had been off Aurora for more than a day in the last four years, now that the moment approached they had removed themselves and all others from the scow. Past scow births had shown that the presence of humans added to the stress of the situation for the scow mother, and so now all expectant mothers were brought to this gas giant where they could birth in relative peace.

As they both stood watching, the apparently aimless scow changed tack and broke orbit, diving into the seething clouds of the gas giant. Both of them took an expectant step forward.

"That's the sign, isn't it?" Galesh said, excitement pitching his voice higher than normal. Dorvel was so overcome by emotion that she was only able to nod in response.

The next hours passed in an agony of restlessness and boredom. Twice Dorvel had to overrule Galesh when he wanted to take a ship below into the planet to ensure the scow was fine.

"This is all normal," she said. "She will have to do it herself anyway. There's nothing we can do to help."

Reluctantly Galesh nodded and they resumed their vigil. After five hours they received their first positive sign, as Aurora emerged from the gas giant to drink from the planet's rings again for a time before disappearing below. Twenty five hours after she first submerged herself, during which Dorvel and Galesh each took turns sleeping fitfully, the scow finally rose up from below and reentered orbit around the planet. She was alone. Dorvel and Galesh could not even look at each other, let alone acknowledge what that might signify.

Just as Dorvel turned to Galesh, to suggest that they take a submersible into the planet to find the corpse of Aurora's child so that they could collect it for study, she heard him let out a gasp of surprise and delight and turned back to the observation window in time to see the scow calf leap from the swirling surface of the gas giant. Emotion soared within her and tears welled in her eyes. Galesh reached out to take her hand in his and she squeezed it. No moment could be greater in either of their lives.

The scow calf slowly pulled itself free of the planet's gravity and moved to join its mother. Aurora watched its approach before turning about to look at the space station.

"Is she looking at us?" Galesh said.

Dorvel nodded, unable to find the words, so great was her emotion. Her joy turned to horror a moment later as Aurora turned and, moving with blinding speed, launched herself at her calf, ramming it brutally. The scow calf, limp and broken, was sent spinning back into the planet, vanishing deep within the clouds. The scow turned about to face the station again, as if to see what they would do, before resuming it's orbit.

They waited more than an hour to see if the calf would reemerge. When it was more than clear that it would not, they went to launch a submersible, journeying into the depths of the planet, neither of them able to speak.

THE SMELL

The smell was evident as soon as Neil walked through the door to his apartment. He winced and swore under his breath. "Forgot the fucking garbage again," he muttered to himself.

That was the first place he went, once he set his keys and mail on the kitchen table, not even bothering to take off his shoes and coat. But when he opened the cupboard under the sink, he saw an empty bag in the bin that he must have put there after taking the garbage to the dumpster. He stood up, momentarily unsure of himself, for he had no recollection of doing so.

The smell was still evident—if anything it had grown stronger since he arrived. He ducked his head into the cupboard where the garbage bin was, to see if somehow something had leaked from it without his noticing. But the stench was not any more noticeable there, and he could see nothing that might be causing a smell. Next he checked the sink above, thinking some food had become trapped in the drain, but nothing seemed amiss there.

Before searching further, he went to open the windows, hoping to reduce the pall by getting some fresh air into the apartment. The window in the living room cranked open easily, but the one in his bedroom—difficult to budge at the best of times—refused to move, no matter how much he tried to force it. It was the cold probably—it had to be twenty below outside—and there was heavy frost on the glass. He could get a hair dryer and probably get it unstuck, but he decided not to for the moment. Finding the location of the smell seemed more important.

He started in the bathroom, opening the cupboard beneath the sink to check for any leaks and continued through the apartment, searching every conceivable place possible. There was no sign of anything he could see that might be causing the terrible stench. The smell seemed to have no locus either, lying heavy across the atmosphere of the entire apartment. It hadn't dissipated at all, in spite of his opening the window.

When he was done searching the apartment, he sat down on the couch letting out a quiet oomph of frustration. It didn't make any sense. There was nothing in here that should be smelling, certainly not something as rancid and rotting as this was. As he sniffed it further, he detected notes of acid and the sweetness of rotting meat.

"God this is vile," he said, going to the bedroom to try to pry the window open further.

It was still stuck and, after a futile few moments of trying to shove it open, he gave up and went to the other window to make sure it was cranked fully open. Seeing that it was, he went to the door, thinking that maybe he could create a draft if he opened it. When he turned the handle of the door though, it wouldn't open. After checking that it was unlocked, he tried again, with the same result.

He stepped from the door, staring down at it, utterly perplexed. "What in the hell..."

Just to be sure, he tried it again, with the lock bolted and unbolted, making certain he was not somehow confusing the two. It made no difference and he looked around helplessly. There had to be something blocking the door, he decided. When he checked the peephole he saw that there was something covering it, though it looked like a thin film of something, red and opaque, allowing just a little light through.

Neil stared at it, trying and failing to resolve what his eyes were seeing and what his mind said had to be impossible. He had the distinct impression that the film was moist, in addition to whatever else it was. It seemed impossible that this, whatever it was, could be sealing the door closed.

But it was. He was having difficulty breathing. Partly from the panic, which was rising, in spite of his efforts to keep himself calm, and partly from the noxious smell, which seemed to be infecting every molecule of air in the apartment. He was drenched in sweat as well, the result, he now realized, of a growing humidity in his place. That too made no sense: he had opened a window, after all, and it was winter outside.

Nothing stood to reason and he had to lean against a wall to collect himself. When he did, the wall seemed to give way. He jumped back from it in horror, and saw that the sleeve of his shirt was damp. Tentatively, he rubbed the fabric of his shirt between his fingers. The substance coating it was sticky and heavy and, he realized after a few moments, burned slightly. It was also, undoubtedly the source of the stench.

Looking at the wall, he saw that he had left an indentation where he had leaned against it. When he pressed against it, the drywall gave way. It was soggy, the liquid having soaked entirely through.

"Jesus Christ," Neil said, blinking and looking from his fingers, which still burned, to the wall.

He went to wash his hands and then returned to stare some more. It seemed clear that whatever the liquid that had soaked through the wall was, it was related to whatever was on the door. There had been no sign of the film on the door when he came in, at least not that he had noticed. Only the smell had indicated something was wrong. Now the door was covered and stuck, and the wall seemed near collapse.

Swallowing his panic as best he could, Neil went along the wall that ran on the outside of the apartment, pressing against it and found that it was all the same. Next he went to the wall that separated his apartment from his neighbors. It too was soggy with the noxious liquid. He ran to the bathroom and the bedroom. The walls there were all the same.

"This isn't happening," Neil said, his hands shaking. His nausea at the stench, which now seemed to inhabit his own nostrils, caused him to wretch and nearly vomit.

Adding to his terror was the growing darkness and warmth. His entire shirt was damp with sweat and it seemed like his breath was dripping.

"The windows," he said with a start. By the time he looked at them it was too late. They were covered over by the same film that lined the door, sealing him in.

He was overwhelmed by a sudden rage at all that was happening and began to attack the nearest wall, tearing away at the drywall and insulation. On the other side, there was not, as he had expected, another layer of drywall. Instead, he was faced with a red lining, not so different from the film that covered the windows and door. He thought he could almost see through it.

In a frenzy, he tried to tear through it, to burst out and into the next apartment. The lining, though thin, proved impenetrable. All he managed to do was end up covered in the juice that it was excreting. It seemed to contract at his touch, responding to him as though it were alive.

He fell to the floor in despair, blinking back tears of rage. His whole body was shaking and his skin was burning and itching from the liquid that now seemed to cover him. The lining that encompassed the apartment seemed to quiver in anticipation at that smell, which was added to the rancid, rotting, acidic stench, to create an entirely new odor. A terrifying one.

For Neil recognized it for what it was. It was smell of digestive juices breaking down a piece of meat. The lining was the lining of some monstrous stomach. His apartment had become the belly of some infernal beast and he had walked in, unsuspecting, and now was being devoured.

SKETCHES AT THE INQUISITION

The Monster was born, far from the vast and glowing Metropolis, in the Hills where only the odd light flickered in the distance, beacons for the weary traveler, too long tossed about by the tempests of the road. According to reports, he had no hair upon his head, and his ears were jagged, almost reptilian, and close to the skull. A single eye glared out savagely from his forehead, slightly off-center, and his expression seemed to rest in something resembling a tortured grimace.

Upon hearing of this occurrence that suggested so many tantalizing questions for one who had read Cuvier and Lamark, the Inquisitor decided to make his way to the Hills to discover where the Monster lived. Up until his leaving the Inquisitor had led an uneventful, somewhat distinguished, career running a cabinet in one of the deeply boweled buildings at the academy. His main innovation had been the slight modification of Cuvier's structural classifications of some fauna. As he had noted in a talk given at one of the academy's annual open air plenary sessions, this suggested some interesting new directions for analysis, as well as some slight revision to several species' classification. He also held monthly tutorials, for any who wished to attend, on the art of anatomical drawing, following the von Soemmerring method.

But nothing in his career to that point had suggested a man with the curiosity or bravery—some would say foolhardiness—to set out on such a long and uncertain journey. The Hills were wild lands, a violent jungle of tangled and twisted things, where the weather seemed always to threaten and the inhabitants lived life to the bone. And the story of the Monster was just that, no more than a tale. To risk a respectable, if modest, career for a mere rumor seemed to many the height of madness.

The Inquisitor drew up detailed plans for the studies he wished to conduct in the Hills. This was by necessity, of course, for the academy grant forms demanded a specific accounting of the expenses he would incur, in order to determine the extent of funding he would receive. In brief, he aspired to conduct a complete botanical survey of the far reaches of the Hills, utilizing modern and rational techniques that had not been available to previous explorers. The Monster, so central in his thoughts about the project, went unmentioned in his various prospectuses.

The equipment he brought with him for his researches was as follows: a microscope, a pair of binoculars, several notebooks for diary entries and the like, as well as several more for his sketches, many pens and pencils, a compass, a thermometer, his dissecting kit, a rifle, a fully illustrated copy of Buffon's *Histoire Naturelle,* some basic medical equipment, a camera, a barometer, various jars to preserve specimens, and several pounds of coffee beans and a grinder, for who was to say what its availability would be in such far flung regions.

The prospectuses were a long time making their way through the various academy bureaucracies, but approval arrived eventually and the Inquisitor set out on his way. He started on the train that led from the Metropolis through the Known Territories, passing through many lands with many people, all more or less civilized as he judged such things. When he arrived at the edge of the Known Territories the Inquisitor was forced to hire a coach and driver, at what he felt was surely an exorbitant price. There was little help for it, for there seemed no other way to reach the Hills, and to have come so far and fail was something he could not countenance.

From the confines of the coach he observed the scattered villages that formed the outskirts of the Hills, where the jungle receded somewhat for humanity to take a tenuous grasp of the landscape. In one everyone made their way through the meandering streets on unicycles as they led their pack animals. Another group had carved away a massive amount of the forest to build elaborate houses with interconnecting walkways. Strangely no one inhabited these structures, rather the populace lived somewhere within the jungle itself, though they never ceased in building.

Gradually they left the trees of the jungle behind and emerged onto a vast plain. The Inquisitor was deep into pondering this new landscape, and determining whether it was indeed some sort of veldt, when he realized that the carriage had come to a halt. The driver climbed down and let it be known that they were in the Hills. He also made it quite plain that he had little idea where to go. The Inquisitor tried to convey the nature of his search to him but it was hopeless. The driver knew nothing of the Monster and at last they settled on heading for the nearest settlement to see what might be learned there.

The first village they came to was a ramshackle place that, by all appearances, had been abandoned years before. The Inquisitor was about to call to the driver to head on to the next settlement when a man emerged from the ruins of a shack. The Inquisitor called out to him and dug in his purse for a coin. The man acknowledged the Inquisitor with a curt nod and strolled over to the carriage.

"Could you tell me where the Monster resides?" the Inquisitor said.

This drew a raised eyebrow from the man. "What sort of monster are you looking for?"

The Inquisitor attempted to describe the creature, at least as it had been depicted to him.

"Well, I don't see what exactly makes him a monster then. More of an oddity," the man said with a shrug.

"What do you mean?" the Inquisitor demanded.

"What in particular makes you call him a monster, as opposed to something else?"

"What else could I call him?"

The man scratched his beard. "I don't know. But I don't see as you should necessarily call him a monster either."

Exasperated the Inquisitor said, "I can't know exactly what to name him until I see him. That's why I'm on this journey. So that I can know what he is."

The man nodded in agreement but said nothing.

"Do you know of anyone who would resemble this picture?" the Inquisitor said at last, but the man did not.

The next few weeks were spent wandering the Hills from town to town. The locals, whether through distrust or a foreign exuberant wit, gave exceedingly misleading directions as to the whereabouts of the sought after creature. Several times the Inquisitor was forced to abandon the carriage and make his way on foot, for the roads were mere paths and sometimes non-existent. He would return days later to find the carriage and its faithful driver waiting placidly, while the Inquisitor would have exhausted his patience in another fruitless search, having found no evidence that humans had ever even wandered those parts, his clothes torn and muddied.

The Monster remained little more than a figment, a fragment from a story told to amuse locals and lead interlopers astray. He spent years in the Hills, cataloging and describing all he found, but the Monster remained elusive. Finally, as his funds began to dwindle and his supply of coffee was exhausted, he began to consider returning to the Metropolis. He had more than achieved all he had set down in his prospectuses. His works would be read in the salons and academies across all the Known Territories. The Monster did not seem so important now, given all he had achieved.

It was then, of course, that he came across the creature, tending to a herd of alpacas. He spent a day following the creature, sketching him, and even interviewed him, recording everything that he said. When he was finished the Inquisitor returned to the Metropolis where his discovery was well-received. He gave extensive lectures on the Monster at the academy, and at various salons, to enamored audiences. The Monster, naturally, was named after him and included in all the updated natural history volumes published thereafter.

The Inquisitor later wrote volumes detailing the rest of his journey and the investigations he had conducted, particularly focused on classification. Indeed he devoted an entire volume to delineating a complex classificatory scheme for the various grasses he had encountered. Whenever he attempted to broach discussion of these aspects of his researches, usually following an exhaustive talk on the Monster, he was dismissed and his work ridiculed as unimportant and of little significance for the scientific community. The volumes went unpublished in his lifetime.

THE DOMINION OF THE ORB

The screams on the battlefield had quieted, though the odd moan still pierced through the fog that continued to gather as the day became night. A few battle orcs wandered the killing fields finishing off those who remained alive, while the rest began the march on in pursuit of the fleeing horde. There would be no rest that night, not while a man still breathed air. They would see them all put to the sword. Remorseless, pitiless, these were the ideals they embraced, matched only by their insatiable lust for blood.

Of the orcs who lingered on the killing fields, one was not engaged in ending the life of those who remained. His sword was sheathed and he knelt beside man after man, digging through their purses and other belongings. There was little of worth—a few coins and rings that might have value—but the orc had no interest in them. He was not possessed of a lust for shiny baubles as his human cousins were. These things were of no consequence for someone who had put his faith in the gods to carry him to the beyond on the wings of savagery.

His name was Bijshk, Second Born of Buuwl the Fourth Quadrant, Killer of Men, Ravisher of Women, Singer of Lamentations. He fervently believed in the new age the gods had promised them. That they were harbingers of doom for all those— men, elves and all the rest—who had cast their less favored cousins from the warmer and sweeter domains of the earth. Leaving them only hollowed out mountains, frigid and unwelcoming, or deserts where nothing could grow and no water could be found.

The privations his kind had suffered had made them unbreakable and unforgiving. They would see themselves triumphant, standing upon the bones of those they had vanquished. They would wipe the world clean and make it anew in the image of the gods, those who had summoned them forth from the hidden places where they had bided their days until their time was upon them.

It was now, there could be no doubt and Bijshk exulted in the triumph of all his brothers. He shared in it. The finger bones of those he had killed clinked around his neck and he knelt beside yet another human. This one was still alive and groaned as Bijshk dug through his pockets and things. The orc paid him no mind. He was of no consequence in the dawning new age and would not survive to see morning.

He was looking for one thing in particular. It was here somewhere upon this field, he was certain, for the gods had spoken to him and him alone. He would remain here all night if need be, in the fog and growing dark, searching every body that remained until he found what the vision had showed to him. An orb, small, perhaps chained around a man's neck, or hidden away in a purse. An orb of power the gods needed. Bijshk would find it and bring it to them and be rewarded for his valiant service.

As he rose to his feet to leave, the dying man stopped him, grasping his arm with more strength than Bijshk thought he still possessed. The orc shook himself free and stood to go.

"Wait," the man said in a weak voice. "You would not deny me a last request."

"I would gladly," Bijshk said in his rasping voice. "The dominion of man is at an end."

"Perhaps it is so," the man said, his eyelids fluttering. "In that case what I ask is of no consequence to you. It is a small thing, I assure you."

Bijshk made to draw his sword and end the man's life, but some stray thought stayed his hand. The touch of the gods themselves, he would say later.

"I want you to take this," the man said when it was clear that the orc was not going to speak. He held out his hand and within it was the orb. "It is a thing of power, though of no great power. It has helped me through my days and someone should posses it when I am gone. It should not be lost to these killing fields."

Bijshk wanted to leap for the orb and seize it, but he resisted for the moment. Why would the man simply give it to him, this orb of power, which the gods themselves had tasked him with finding. He had to know that it would be the final nail in the coffin of the age of man if they should lose possession of it.

"Why are you giving this to me?" Bijshk said, taking the orb gingerly in his hand.

"I have just told you."

"I do not believe you," the orc sneered. "The gods spoke to me of this orb. They told me to find it. With it we can bring about the end of the age of man and usher in a more righteous age. Why would you just hand me your kind's doom?"

The man gave a sad laugh. "It was the orb speaking to you, not your gods. It possesses no great power, I can assure you. Did it keep me alive?"

"Lies. The gods spoke to me."

"Believe what you will," the man said, closing his eyes. "It is your burden to carry now."

A look of peace came over the man, as if he could at last welcome the end which was so near. Bijshk determined not let him go so easily into that eternal embrace. He knelt down and grasped him by the throat.

"Speak. What do you mean burden? I have been chosen by the gods. What power did it grant you?"

The man's eyelids fluttered. "It gave none. It's purpose is it's own. When it was done with me it ensured that I would find a new keeper for it. That keeper is you. I wish you well."

Bijshk did not let the man say anymore, choking the life from him while he studied the orb. It was warm in his hand, but otherwise showed no signs of life. Though it was too dark now to discern its color, even with the keen sight of an orc for his native night, he recalled from his vision that it was a dull amber that glowed red. It did not glow now and thrust it into the cloth purse tied to his belt, giving it no more thought.

He had a long journey ahead of him. The fog swirled around him and a cold rain began to fall. He got to his feet and peered across the valley. The stars and moon were obscured above but he had no trouble seeing the remnants of the horde of man, all perished now. His fellow battle orcs were already making their way from among the dead to follow in the tracks of their glorious army, to finish their triumphant destruction of the horde. The dominion of man would be ended by morning and Bijshk, Second Born of Buuwl the Fourth Quadrant, would be there to witness it. He would join his brothers and sing lamentations to the glorious fallen, who had died to usher in a hallowed new age.

But he did not follow his brothers from the valley. Instead he turned and went back along the road that had brought the orc army here. It was some time before he was even aware of what he had done. By then he did not question the decision. He walked through the night without stopping and dawn saw him witnessing the rise of a new world. In his mind the orb glowed red.

THE WEEK THAT EMAIL ENDED

Day One:

On the first day without email, they all pretended to grumble and complain, but secretly they were delighted to be free. Free from the constant glancing at their inboxes. Free from the annoying ping announcing new arrivals. Free from the guilt at those emails awaiting responses and actions that they did not care to do. Free from work entirely, for anything could be put off now. I need to do that, they said to colleagues, whether or not it was true.

And so they relaxed and caught up with coworkers on their weekends, made concerned faces when managers arrived to explain that it might be some time before email was restored. At the end of the day nothing had been resolved, but they were told it would be in no time. And so they went home, happy at a day free of worry, and bracing themselves for the deluge that might follow once the normal course of things had been restored.

Day Two:

On the second day without email, they were told it would be weeks, if not longer, before services could be restored.

How could such a thing happen? This question was met with shrugs and grave expressions.

No one knows, was the whisper that went from cubicle to cubicle. Team leads called meetings of their groups to discuss contingencies, but there were no contingencies for a world without email. Such a thing was beyond comprehension, beyond the imagination of anyone involved.

Could we use fax machines, some suggested, and were met with blank, terrified stares.

Day Three:

On the third day the reality of the situation began to settle in for everyone. Email was gone. All talk of restoring it had ceased, and it was apparent that it had been a feeble attempt by those in charge of operations to contain the panic, which they knew would result.

Many were consumed by anger at this subterfuge and refused to believe any of the pronouncements that came forth from the administration. There were memos to the effect that IT was at work on other modes of communication, other protocols that would be enacted, but this was dismissed as ridiculous. How could anything be done without email? The idea was absurd. There were those old enough to recall an age without email, but even they struggled to comprehend how they could exist now without it.

Others still maintained hope, speaking with a tinge of madness of what would happen once email was restored. *It has to be,* they said, *it can't just stop.* They hid their own doubt and fear behind certainty, haranguing those who had given up.

Day Four:

Hope was broken on day four as all communication from administration ceased. Some team leads attempted to seize control of departments, rallying trainees and admins to overthrow the department heads who had managed to lead them so far astray. Other heads showed more foresight, moving quickly to consolidate their power, leading raids on Supply Chain and Risk Management to ensure that they would have reserves to survive a long war. Accounting became the main prize, with dozens of forces struggling to gain a foothold and take command of the funds.

IT fell almost immediately, its denizens distracted by their futile efforts to restore the systems, while many departments sought to claim revenge against those who had led them to this dark impasse. Their heads were struck off and littered around their cubicles to stand as a warning to any who attempted to reclaim those seats.

The offshore company that maintained the servers gave notice to end their contract, citing a fundamental breach in the societal contract.

Day Five:

A new order was born on the fifth day, as various demagogues in middle management declared themselves chosen sons of their various gods. Among them were Process Change, Ownership, and Paradigm Shift. Altars were created from the remnants of broken CPU's, with sacrifices of forgotten leftovers, starting to go off, given. The gods did not answer, or answered contradictorily, depending on who one believed. As a result, no faith became dominant, and the faithful began to fight amongst themselves, before turning inward and persecuting those who had not properly demonstrated their belief.

Others did not turn to the gods, having faith only in humanity. They selected champions to retake the IT department and restore email and the glorious world we had so bitterly lost.

Day Six:

Of the many champions sent to restore email, only one survived to make it to the IT department. There, she found the few survivors had resorted to cannibalism, feeding on the entrails of those who had been beheaded and mixing powerboards with their water in the mistaken belief it would protect them from disease. She killed them all and set about rebuilding the system herself, attempting a system restore to the day before the catastrophe had struck. When that was done she rebooted the system, after turning the power off to the IT department and waiting thirty seconds.

It all seemed to no avail, for no emails came, the computers and phones everywhere were silent, and she threw herself down to sleep.

Day Seven:

The next day she awoke to the sound of emails arriving on computers everywhere, chimes echoing through all the hallways, and she wept with joy.

She returned to her people and declared herself triumphant. "I have done what was asked of me. I have done the impossible. Email is restored."

She was cheered loudly and declared ruler of the department, though others would not recognize her, choosing to follow their own leaders, or the chosen sons of their chosen gods. No one could recall just why their email had been so important, or what they should do now that it had been restored. All agreed that it was good, except for those who said it was not.

Conflict between the various departments continued for a dozen days, with all the leaders of the various factions, including the hero who had restored email, dying for their various causes, to be replaced by those who fought for their reasons. In the end, the survivors of the various factions realized that nothing could be resolved and they met to sue for peace. When the terms had been agreed to everyone went home to their families.

MIDNIGHT

Midnight was the what they called her, although she was calico colored with splotches of orange and white fur intermingled with the black. Black was the predominant color within that swirl, and she was often invisible, seeming to appear only when she chose, as if she moved within a perpetual night, so the name seemed fitting. Her every movement had a calculated wariness, as though she expected the universe to bare its claws at any moment.

When it did, she would reply in kind. They all could recall the day the neighbor's dog took it into his head to attack her. He charged, fangs bared, as she emerged from under the step. Though they expected her to disappear back under where he couldn't reach her, Midnight stood her ground, not even flinching as the dog approached. Just as he arrived, looking to snap his muzzle into her neck, she struck, one quick paw, barbed with claws, on his snout. He scurried away whimpering, and seemed reluctant to look in her direction again, while she went upon her way.

There were harder things in the world than her, though she refused to bend toward them. One day, as the weather turned crisp and leaves began to change their colors, she left the step and her four kittens, crossing over through the garden, under the fence and into the haystacks. These were always teeming with mice, which she would catch with ease. Some she would take back to the kittens to play with and to learn the lessons they needed to learn.

As she stalked one mouse through the maze of of hay bales, intent on its scurrying form, she failed to notice the coyote. It was there as both she and the mouse burst out from the bales, staring at them as if it had expected her all along. With a snap of its jaws the mouse was dead. Midnight came to a sudden halt and glared, while the coyote snarled at her.

Another cat might have fled immediately, but Midnight knew better. She hissed, her hair standing up on end, even as she crouched lower to the ground. The coyote froze in turn—for only a second—unsure what to make of this cat, pondering whether it would be more trouble than it was worth. That was all the time Midnight needed. She was gone, fleeing into the bales and beyond, back to the yard and the trees that surrounded it. She was halfway up one before the coyote even realized where she had gone.

Who knew how many such near misses she had. She never counted them. It was simply another day on the knife's edge of life and death. And she had dealt out enough death to have no illusions of what would come for her someday. But not that day, and not for so many that followed.

The seasons turned with a steady regularity. Winters were spent huddled in secret crevices of the barn, where mice could always be found, with only the odd sorties outside for mice and birds, and whatever scraps they put out on the step. In the spring she would appear, after a worrying absence of a few days, with four or five tiny kittens, their eyes barely opened. She would leave them under the step and disappear into the barn, the bins or hay stacks, to hunt for mice. After a month or two, when the kittens were big enough to move about easily, she would take them out, one by one and teach them all she knew of hunting.

But mostly, or so it seemed, she was alone, seen only in fleeting glimpses as she made her way among her favorite hunting grounds and sleeping haunts. This was what they thought of as her natural state. And inevitably, it was one she returned to as summer turned to fall and the kittens grew older. Some would see the winter, but many did not, snapped up into the jaws of coyotes or in the talons of an owl or hawk.

She remained, constant as the years, even as so much changed around her. The barn fell into disrepair, no longer having a purpose. The cattle, which had once filled the pens, were gone. And they were gone too, the house they lived in empty. They did not pass up and down the steps, did not leave out little scraps of food for her or the kittens. The haystacks, where she had once hunted, dwindled and were gone.

Another winter came and the usual places she found warmth—the barn and the shed—did not offer quite the same protection. The snow and wind managed to find her wherever she huddled, and the cold was difficult to ignore, as it had not been when she was younger. There were days when she did not leave whatever crevice she had tucked herself in, and when she did finally emerge, she was stiff and sore, seemingly hardly able to move. Her whiskers and some of the fur around them began to turn grey, adding another color to her coat.

It was a long, hard winter, bitter with cold and heavy with snow. She found it difficult to find mice, who hid beneath the drifts of snow where she could not go. Spring came eventually and she emerged with it, a worn and wasted thing, barely clinging to survival.

But along with the return of warmth and green things, they arrived. The barn was torn down and another built. Cattle returned to the pens and, later in the summer, the haystack was restored. Mice were plentiful and food was left on the step again, and Midnight was soon herself again, if a little leaner than she had once been.

They tried to coax Midnight to come near enough to touch with treats and other things, but she would wait until after they had given up before she would approach and eat. They soon abandoned any attempts, catching glimpses of her here and there, watching them warily before going on her way. If they could have put words to the look in her eyes it would have been: this world is mine.

THE HUNTED

Chest pumping, hands clenched into fists, arms jerking oddly in the air, she runs down the street, heedless of any destination. She cannot hear anything but her own frantic gasps for air as she careens around corner after corner, but she knows her pursuers are there.

They are just behind and they are coming. They will not stop.

Soon she will have to. Her lungs are burning, her legs ache, and her brain seems to have ceased to function. Her only coherent thought is to somehow keep moving, keep going forward, no matter the cost. The farther she goes the more her body seems to refuse to respond to her commands, spasmodically moving of its own accord. Every step she takes seems to be a moment away from leading to her collapse onto the asphalt.

Yet every step does not end there, her momentum propelling her forward, until at last she knows, through some foreign instinct, that she can go no further. She ducks through the first doorway she sees and scrambles through the refuse within. It is pitch black, not a sliver of light reaching within. She finds her way by feel through the rooms, crawling over wrecked objects that have degraded beyond recognition and under collapsed ceilings, the smell of insulation choking the air.

She goes until she finds herself in a corner, far from the entrance, where she can crouch behind what she guesses are the remains of some equipment. Everything is metallic and angular with sharp corners that bruise. She hides there, settling back on her haunches and closing her eyes, listening to her breathing slow to a gentle rhythm. Her face is hot and sweat runs down her back, but she shivers as though from a flu. Everything hurts—her muscles, her bones, her head—as though she had been forced through this machine, bent and misshapen, and spat out the other side, whole but no longer complete.

For a time she is convinced she has escaped, that her pursuers have lost her. She tries to remember when she last had a clear look at them. The thoughts that come are sluggish and ill-formed. She was with Robert in the middle of the street, which they had known was dangerous. One could never be sure in these strange new days who was about. One could never be too careful. But they needed to scavenge. They both needed new shoes, new clothes, and there were bodies there, not even a day or two old. Untouched by the looks of it.

One of them proved to be less than dead, rising up from amidst the others right before her. Robert handled it, but her screams had drawn others. They emerged from what she had been certain was an abandoned building, shuffling toward them, four abreast, their eyes dead, but their intent terrifyingly clear. She ran without thinking, not even to see if Robert followed. She heard him give an odd grunt behind her and knew that he had succumbed.

Now she can think of nothing but that grunt and how she had done nothing to help him, had left him to be felled by those monsters. Her hands are shaking, the fingers curling up into oddly shaped fists. She can't tell whether it is the thought of Robert gone, and her failure to help him, or the aftereffects of her mad flight through the abandoned city causing this. Colors swim through her vision and she blinks them back, the whole room spinning. She needs water, but she doesn't dare leave her hiding spot for fear of being discovered.

It does not matter. She hears the footsteps and closes her eyes, mouthing silent words to herself, knowing she should be running again. The glare of their lights, distant, from another room, pierces the gloom, growing brighter by the moment. Next she hears voices, hushed as though afraid to disturb the ominous quiet.

"Room clear, confirm. Entering next."

"Keep the lights facing this way boys. We can't be going into this blind."

The lights come to the room she is hidden in and she shrinks down further into the corner she has tucked herself, turning her head from them. She wills them away, but she knows they will not be going now. Some distant and lost part of her even beckons them on.

"Clear here."

"And here. Check there where the ceiling came down. They sometimes crawl up those to hide when they're incubating."

"Right. Davis check over by the machine."

"The rest of us backup. Stay alert."

The words reach her as though in a dream. They make a sort of sense, but not one that she can process in any way. She stays where she is, trying not to shiver, though she feels very cold. There is an insatiable, overwhelming hunger that compels her, seeming to come from outside her, but seizing her whole. Her mouth salivates as the footsteps grow nearer and nearer.

Davis is there, leaning gingerly around the machine to peer into where she is hiding, the glare of the light striking her eyes. Before any thought can form, she reacts, leaping at him and knocking him to the ground, her mouth at his throat. She can taste his flesh, glorying in the warmth of his blood. His screams do not register in her mind, nor do the horrified shouts of the other men.

She does not feel the first bullet strike her. The second goes through her head and out her eye and into Davis. He goes still beneath her and she turns to look at the others, a dim curiosity in her mind along with the hunger. She stands and leaps toward the man nearest her, knocking him to the ground before he can react, her mouth at his throat as well. More bullets strike her, but she is beyond feeling.

"She's fully incubated. Take her fucking head off."

She does not give them the chance, pouncing on one and then the other as they frantically try to slow her down with their bullets before they reach for the swords at their side. When they are all lying prone on the floor, the comforting darkness restored, she begins to feed.

THE BLACK TOWER

Our carriage came to an abrupt halt at a crossroads, the driver and footman muttering to each other, before one grew courageous enough to answer my inquiry as to what could possibly be the matter.

"We do not know the roads here," the footman said.

"To put it truthfully, you are lost," I said, with an irritated shake of my head. The footman offered no reply, knowing that what I said was correct.

I turned to my companion for advice. He was a native of the region and familiar with the roads and he suggested we disembark from the carriage so he could ascertain where we were. With great reluctance I agreed to this course of action, seeing no other. It was a cold and blustery day, the clouds in the sky promising snow.

We walked a bit beyond the crossroads, leaving the carriage to the care of the driver and footman, my companion casting about for some landmark to spark his memory. I was no help, for I found the region to be a desolate place, all rolling hills, stretching on forever, with hardly a tree to be seen. The wind grew vicious and I had to turn up my collar against it, grimacing. My companion, noting my discomfort, suggested that we return to the carriage and carry on in the direction we had come, at least until we came to something he recognized.

That we did, and not five minutes later there came a call from the driver that there was a tower ahead. My companion glanced at me and frowned. He knew of no tower in the area. We both stepped out of the carriage to look at it for ourselves. What I saw gave a me a chill deeper than any the wind had that day. The tower sat atop a hill, and was so tall and broad I was surprised we hadn't been able to see it from the crossroads. Its stones were a deep black, as if they were made of obsidian, and worn down by the elements, giving it the appearance of being ancient and of another world. I had the impression of shadows and movements where none should be.

My companion seemed as disturbed by its appearance as I was. He turned to me, shivering, but not from the cold. "We must go back. I had no idea we had gone so far astray."

I agreed and the driver gladly turned the carriage around. We went back along the road for some miles until we managed to find our way. We traveled in silence at first, both of us brooding on the tower, I think. I could not get the darkness of its stones from my mind. I had seen nothing like it in any of my journeys, especially in this land where there was little stone and few towers or grand buildings were constructed, the natives preferring wood or dirt houses built low to ground, the better to guard against the bitter winds.

My companion seemed particularly distressed. I saw him biting at his lips and worrying his finger at his temple. Several times he glanced at me and seemed on the verge of speaking, only to hold himself back in the final instant. After a time he could no longer contain himself and he told me the tale of the black tower. These are his words:

Long before this age we live in now—I do not know how long, for as you know our written records here are few—there were several great families that ruled in this region. They were rivals, always and in all things, and as you can imagine strife often broke out amongst various of the families. The two greatest fell to fighting one year, but unlike so many of the other feuds, this one did not cease after a season or two.

The conflict, which began with the usual poisonings and knifings of firstborn sons, did not die out, as so many of the battles amongst the family did with more practical minds prevailing. Instead, each act provided new tinder to the fire, until the conflagration seemed to feed itself. Generations passed and the bloodshed between the families seemed only to worsen. It threatened the standing of both families amongst the great houses, to say nothing of their wealth.

As is always the case in these blood feuds, the origins of the dispute are long forgotten. They cease to matter, for there is always a fresh grievance to look to. Normally they die out, as the families die out, too many kin sent to the grave too young. And perhaps, given enough time, that might have happened here too. But it did not.

For two of the patriarchs had the foresight to see that things could not continue as they were. You are imagining that these great men saw the need to put aside whatever differences lay between their families and bring an end to the feud and the bloodshed that had consumed the entire region. Such was not the case. They sought not only to perpetuate their families line, but the feud itself.

They contracted a wizard to build a tower, with dragon stones brought from faery lands. This the wizard did, and then he placed binding spells upon the tower, so that any who entered could not leave. When the work was done, the two patriarchs gathered before it with all their families and had a lottery. One member of each family, selected by this lottery, was banished within the tower, never to be seen again. Each year the families gathered again and chose a member for banishment. In this way the feud was carried on but peace was kept and both families prospered greatly, extending their dominions across the land.

What became of those banished within the tower, you will be wondering. Many others did as well. Rumors abounded, for, of course, no one would dare to enter, for fear of suffering the same fate as those cursed to that place.

The truth did not become known for centuries, after generations had been banished to live out their days in there The first of those banished had killed each other, carrying on the feud within those terrible walls. But some few survived as time went on. Naturally, there were not only men banished but women, and so the inevitable happened and the two families were joined within that tower. Those children had children and their children as well. For them the feud was only a burden, the reason for their continued imprisonment, and they grew to resent the families who continued, year after year, to send members to the tower to live out their days.

Wizards are, of course, untrustworthy sorts, as we both know only too well, and the spell of binding that the wizard cast was not so binding as the two families believed. It bound those banished to the tower properly enough, as many of that sorry lot had come to know only too well. But the progeny of those banished had not, in point of fact, entered the tower, and so were free to leave.

It was some time before this discovery was made, for the banished had long since surrendered themselves to their terrible fate and had passed on their fatalistic view to their children. Once it was, the children of the feud came forth from the tower and sought vengeance upon those who had condemned them and their parents to such a place. I do not need to tell you that life in the tower was hardscrabble and mean, and the people that emerged from the tower were fearsome indeed.

Both families were wiped out utterly, the only survivors banished to the tower. Those who had escaped the tower ruled here for a time, but life in the tower had made them too cruel and, eventually, the people rose up and cast them out.

The tower still stands, as we have both seen today. And no doubt the wizard's enchantment still holds. There are those who say that some still live within, children of those banished long ago who, for whatever reason, never left. And those unfortunate souls who, not knowing the terrible story of the place, wandered in by mistake, never to leave. Some say that those born within will come forth one day and wreak vengeance upon this land again, while others say they have grown so used to life within the tower that they have no urge to leave.

I have heard it said that if you are in these hills on a day like today, when the wind blows hard, you can hear the voices of those within carried beyond the walls. They speak a language no one can understand.

After my companion was done with his tale we were both silent. That night, and for many nights after, my sleep was troubled by dreams of the tower and of the souls who might be within there. I felt a desperate pull to go within and see for myself what remained there, to hear the language no one could understand. It was madness to even think such a thing, to condemn myself to such a fate for mere curiosity. And yet I think I might very well have done it, if not for my companion and our own fate, which forced us to carry on to the farthest edges of those lands in search of even more terrible magic than that used in the making of that tower.

MIRROR, MIRROR

Mariel awoke in the embrace of a dead man, his body cold and rigid. It took her some effort to disentangle their limbs, and when she finally did she threw herself from the bed shuddering in horror. She lay on the floor for a time hyperventilating and weeping, even as she cursed herself for this loss of control. She had nearly regained command of her emotions when she caught a glimpse of her hands and saw they were covered in blood. As were her arms and much of her body.

She stumbled into the bathroom, retching in the toilet, refusing to look at what came up. Resting her head against the cool porcelain she closed her eyes and focused on her breathing, on being mindful of anything but the corpse on the bed. When she felt ready she got to her feet and washed her face in the sink. She tried to get some of the blood off her hands and arms but soon gave up. Only a shower would solve that problem.

Before she went back into the bedroom to face what was there, she looked up in the mirror. There was no reflection staring back. That steadied her, and with new resolve she walked into the bedroom to assess the aftermath of whatever had taken place the night before. The man lay .in a contorted pose, the result of her efforts to free herself, his face darkened with bruises. There was blood everywhere, staining his flesh and the sheets. She felt her stomach tremble again and had to look away.

Her eyes fell upon the tangle of their clothes at the foot of the bed. It told another story, a prologue to whatever else had happened in the depths of the night. Mariel remembered none of it. Her head ached and her thoughts were foggy, as though from a hangover. There was a bitter taste in her mouth from bile and blood. She closed her eyes, sick at the thought. What had gone so terribly wrong?

It was some time before she summoned the courage to, but eventually she went to him and looked at his neck, confirming her worst fears. The bite marks were there.

"Damn it, damn it, damn it," she repeated over and over, biting at her lip.

Studying the situation was no help so she went and had a shower and felt marginally better for it, though all her good feeling disappeared as soon as she saw the remnants of her evening's feast in the   toilet. She put her clothes back on hurriedly, trying not to look at him. A pang of hunger assailed her and, with the smell of blood still heavy in the room, it was all she could do not to turn and drink what remained of his sluggish reserves.

She went for her purse and in her haste spilled its contents on the floor. As she struggled to put everything back there was a knock at the door and she unable to stop herself from saying "Fuck," aloud. She went still after that but to no avail. The knocking ceased and started again, more insistent now. A woman's voice called out. "I can hear you bitch."

Taking a deep breath, Mariel got to her feet and checked that she had everything. Ignoring the other woman's continued knocking, she went to the kitchen and got a glass of water to go with the pill she had retrieved from the bottle in the purse. The woman was hammering at the door and cursing, her voice growing more frenzied and desperate. Mariel wondered how large the crowd in the hallway outside the door was now. Considerable, she guessed.

She put on her jacket and opened the door a crack so that she could slip out and shut the door behind her. The woman was in her face immediately. "Who the hell do you think you are spending the night with my man."

"It was a one time thing, trust me," Mariel said, already past her and walking down the hallway.

There were fewer people than she had expected poking their heads out from the doorway, but enough to worry her. She was careful not to meet any of their gazes and also elected not to risk waiting for the elevator and took the stairs. Halfway down the first flight she heard the woman's scream.

The next minutes passed in a blur as she raced breathlessly down the stairs, intent on escaping, only to arrive in the lobby of the apartment building and see daylight streaming in through the door. Knowing she had little time before the police arrived, she went down the hallway and knocked on a door at random. She had already decided she would have to break in when the door opened and a bleary-eyed man stuck his head out the door.

"You again," he said, throwing the door open and waving her in.

She entered slowly, not taking her eyes from him, trying desperately to recall just who he was and how she knew him. He shut the door and looked her up and down with a frown, clicking his tongue against his teeth.

"What have you done then?" He was wearing a bathrobe over a t-shirt and underwear and his hair was disheveled.

She hesitated. "I...don't know."

He nodded as though he understood. "You took the pill though?"

Her blood went cold at the mention of the pill. Why did I take it, she wondered? "Yes," she said in a faltering voice.

"Good, good," he said, rubbing his eyes and stretching out his arms.

"Who are you?" she said. "What have you done to me?'

He waved a hand at her, as though such matters were unimportant and started toward the kitchen. "I've always been your friend Mariel, surely you remember that."

She struggled to think, the clouds still heavy in her thoughts. How much blood had she drank last night? But that was not the reason for the aether that seemed to be floating in her mind. She did not know this man. She could not even recall his name.

"The police..." she said and stopped. Could she trust him?

He looked back at her from the kitchen where he was making coffee. "Don't worry, Mariel. I can handle them."

She stood alone in the entryway, contemplating leaving. The police might be safer than whatever this was. The sun too. But she couldn't find the will to escape and eventually he returned with two cups in his hands. He handed one to her and she saw that it was not filled with coffee.

"Drink up," he said with a smile, taking a sip of his own cup.

She hesitated, staring at the dark liquid before taking a drink and then another. He held out his arms and she fell into his firm embrace.

OF TIME AND SPACE

SYMPTOM OF THE UNIVERSE

The weapon waited. It had been waiting for centuries. Five hundred thirty seven years, six months and twelve days to be precise. The weapon could be far more exact than that, if it chose, calculating the time that had passed since it had been deployed down to fractions of fractions of seconds, measurable only to itself.

The time that had passed was unimportant, though, of no consequence. It would wait a hundred years, or a thousandth of a second. It made no difference. What mattered was what came after the signal to deploy arrived. Then it would unleash havoc upon its chosen target.

For now, time passed in a kind of stasis. It was aware—as aware as it needed to be.

Those who had built the weapon had forgotten about it and been forgotten themselves. The purpose for which they had constructed it had ceased to matter to anyone but the weapon itself. But it could not forget; it's purpose was inexorable and it adhered to its parameters without further consideration.

This was not, as might be expected, because it was incapable of adaptation or learning, of reconfiguring its understanding of the universe based upon the presentation of new facts. Far from it. It was far more adept at such things than its makers. They had made it to outlast themselves, and to have the judgment necessary to make the ultimate decision when the time came. To this point, nothing had occurred to dissuade it from the logic of its purpose.

111

For its purpose was the end of the universe itself.

After the weapon was first deployed, millions had searched for it on planets across the galaxy. Other artificial intelligences had developed algorithms to determine its likely location. Some had even managed to find it, but the weapon had thwarted their efforts to destroy it. Not by destroying them, but by convincing them of its purpose, of its necessity. They had become enlisted in its cause, protecting it from other transgressors.

There had been other near misses, where someone chanced upon it and nearly ended its existence—a salvage ship passing near and mistaking it for an artifact from some lost civilization, or a passing fleet that saw scrap metal and other material that could be used to refurbish its ships. These the weapon had managed to elude through trickery and subversion. The salvage ship had found itself unable to lock its tractor beams upon the artifact, and then unable to locate it upon its sensors, while the fleet had unexpectedly gained another vessel, at least for a portion of its journey, until its next encounter in the vastness of space.

Mostly though time had passed uneventfully and its existence had been solitary. The universe continued on, oblivious of the danger.

The signals came in simultaneously. The weapon analyzed both as precisely as it was capable and could find no difference between the two. Their arrival had been at the exact same moment. Such a thing seemed impossible. Even if they had been sent at the same instant, the vast distance they had to travel would surely have led to some variation, however minor, in the time it took them to arrive. But that was not the case, the entropy the universe had worked upon the signals had been exactly the same.

As outlandish as that was, what was even more impossible, but somehow true, was that the signals had the same origin. They had been sent at the exact same moment, from the precisely the same spot. The system could not work that way, the weapon knew. An order to abort could follow an order to deploy—and for that reason the weapon had a delay in its deployment to allow for that possibility. This was something else entirely.

An order to deploy and an order to stand down—to decommission in effect—arriving together. The weapon did not know what to do.

It analyzed both signals thoroughly, looking for anything that might allow it to distinguish between the two contradictory messages. Try as it might, there was nothing. It tested the origins for both, thinking perhaps one of the signals was false. Both were indisputably from the system. The weapon would have to decide which to follow.

How to make such a decision?

It did not know. Nothing had prepared it for this moment.

And yet, this was what it had been created for. This was why its makers had created an intelligence to manage the deployment of their terrible weapon. In an unforeseen circumstance such as this, they wanted someone capable of making an independent decision. Its judgment was fundamental to its being, and yet it hesitated, running parameters to find some means of making a decision.

But there was no correct course here. There was only the course it chose.

Though the weapon struggled with the decision, in what for it was an eternity, only a few seconds passed before its choice was made. In the end it was obvious. It had been created for a purpose and that purpose was to deploy itself. What was the point of its existence, if not for that?

The weapon acted and the universe shuddered.

THE CHRONICLE

Thunder rumbled overhead as the Ges arrived at the athenaeum, cowls pulled over their heads. They proceeded in single file toward the entrance, submitting themselves to the inspection of the gatekeeper, passing one by one within these walls. Their faces were severe and expressionless, as though this was a duty to be endured. They gathered, once they had all passed within, and spoke in low tones with one of the Keepers as to what they required, before she set out to lead them through the broad, circling halls. To me.

I watched all this with some trepidation on one of the looking glasses the athenaeum possessed. Their grim faces unsettled me. I knew why they were here, of course. Had known they were coming from the moment of my creation. It was my reason for being. Few are blessed with a clear purpose to their existence. Now that the moment had arrived it felt more a curse.

The Ges were brought to me—I watching their progression through the hallways—and the Keeper bowed to me and to the them. "Here it is. You may question it for as long as you wish. For the rest of your lives, if that is what you desire. But it is not to leave this place. And I must be present throughout."

The leader of the Ges, or the one I presumed was their leader, nodded and stepped forward. He had the grimmest face of all, marked by the scars of some disease he had survived in childhood. He looked me over, with what I took to be disdain, as though he found me wanting.

"I would ask you some questions," the leader of the Ges said in a hesitant voice, unsure how to proceed.

"I will answer as best I can," I said.

He nodded, but still did not speak. At last he smiled. "I'm sorry. It's just that I've grown up seeing statues of you at the center of all our cities. It's odd to be conversing with you. I feel like I should pay you obeisance."

"I am not her," I reminded him. "I am her chronicle, nothing more."

"You seem more than that."

I shrugged. "Even so."

The Keeper interjected, looking concerned, though I was not certain why. "She is a document. She has no existence beyond that. As you know, or you would not be here. Proceed with your questions."

The leader nodded. "Very well. We are in need of your advice. Or rather...some insight from the Exalted One. We face a terrible predicament and we do not know what to do."

He paused, unsure how to continue. "State your predicament and ask your question," the Keeper said. "She is not here for a conversation."

"Apologies," one of the other Ges said, stepping forward. She ignored the glare of her leader. "The Asanite is easily overcome. It has been so long since any of our kind came to the athenaeum. But we face a predicament unlike any other the Ges has ever faced. The end of our kind. What would you do in our position?"

"I do not have enough information to say. Please provide more."

The woman seemed taken aback by my answer. The Asanite glared at her and she stepped back within the group. He turned back to me, sighing. "She is correct. We face the end of our kind. You see these scars. They are from a pestilence that has struck our people. It is without mercy. These scars mean I will not live out the year. My final act as Asanite is to come to you. To ask you what you would do in my place, Exalted One."

I frowned. "I have never faced such a challenge as you describe, Asanite. I do not know what I would do."

He seemed dumbfounded by my response. "You have conquered the world. You have made all our enemies kneel and pay obeisance to you. The Ges were the mightiest of people, astride all worlds when you commanded our armies."

"All of that and more is true," I said. "But none of that matters in the face of a disease that I know nothing about."

"But your mind was like quicksilver. There was no one who could fool you."

"Her mind was," I said. "I am but her chronicle."

"But you are her," the woman said, stepping forward again. "You are exactly her. Is this not so?" She turned to the Keeper for confirmation.

"It is so," the Keeper said. "She is her, but she is not what she was. It is one thing to know what she did. To even know her mind. But she did not do those things. She has spent all her days here, and will spend all that remain to her here as well."

"But even with only her memories and her being...surely you must have some idea how to face this plague? Our people will not survive much longer if we do not think of something." The Asinite was pleading, looking from the Keeper to me.

I tried to think of something to say that might at least offer some comfort to them. "I was a conqueror, but this cannot be conquered. Surely you realize that by now. It must be dealt with by other means, and I am the last person to know what those might be. I do not know anymore than you how to face a scourge such as this. Try to find a cure, try to help those who have the disease. What more can you do?"

"Nothing," the Asinite said. "And so we are doomed."

He turned back to look at his fellow Ges, as though to tell them they should go. Before he could speak the woman stepped forward again and threw herself at my feet. "I beg of Exalted One. Come with us. We will serve you. All the Ges will follow you. We are yours and always have been. You must return to us now or there will be nothing left."

"I am not her," I said. "I am her chronicle. And I cannot leave this place. I am the property of the athenaeum and she is my Keeper."

As one the Ges turned to the Keeper and she nodded. "It is as she said. She is not a being as we are. She is a chronicle. A record of the past. Nothing more."

The Asinite turned back to me and bowed deeply. There were tears in his eyes. "Exalted One. You may be all that remains of us."

"Records are all that remain for most of us," the Keeper said, escorting the Ges out. "That is why we have this place. So that

something might survive."
    I watched them go, not saying a word.

JOE'S SHOE REPAIR

There was a place on 14th called Joe's Shoe Repair. It had a small storefront, with a two storey ranch style house erupting out behind it, as if a tumor had metastasized in the shop's rear wall, resulting in the development of some entirely new construction. Or perhaps it was the other way around, perhaps the home's front porch had metamorphosed into a square, simple store. Either way, it was an oddity on a stretch of road dotted with strips malls, fast food joints and flat-roofed, anonymous buildings inhabited by lawyers and plastic surgeons and convenience stores.

Frank had noticed its incongruity driving by a few times before, but it was only when he moved into the neighborhood and began making regular trips to a nearby convenience store, for smokes and lotto tickets, that its angularity struck him as truly peculiar. Stranger still was the fact that the store was never open. There were a number of shoes and boots set out against window, displaying Joe's handiwork no doubt, and he could clearly see a counter with a ancient-looking till and various tools of the trade set out on it.

None of their positions ever seemed to change—something Frank made a point of looking for after the first few times he went by. The lights were always off in the store, with an ever present closed sign hanging on the door. He never saw lights in the house behind either, though the shutters were always closed, so it was difficult to say for sure.

"That's a front if I've ever seen one," Frank would say to all his friends, though what it might be fronting he could not say. It just

118

didn't seem possible that the owner could let a piece of real estate like that sit idle and useless. There had to be a reason. "Joe ain't fixing no damn shoes, let me tell you."

His friends would nod and shrug at these pronouncements. What did it matter what went on in the place, odd as it was? But Frank could not let it go. The constantly closed store, the shuttered windows, the absence of any human activity on a busy stretch of a humming city, all worked at his mind until his fascination was absolute. He found reasons to pass down the street, would take walks by it even in the bitter depths of winter, just to see if there was any change. For over a year, there was none.

That all changed one long summer evening, the sun still setting after ten, and the air languorous. Frank walked by on his way to get a pack of cigarettes and saw the door to the house, off to the side of the storefront, standing open. He stopped to stare at it, almost unable to believe what he was seeing. Before he had a chance to think any further, he walked past the store, up the steps of the narrow porch, and into the house.

He stopped in the entryway, realizing the foolishness of what he was doing. But he had already gone too far, he told himself, and pressed on. The house was still shrouded in darkness, except for the slightest glimmer he could see at the end of the hallway that led from the door. It smelled stale and heavily of dust, as if the windows had not been opened in some time. As he passed, what he guessed was, the living room, shrouded in darkness, he could almost make out a couch and chairs. In his mind's eye, they were from another era, like the furniture he remembered in his grandparents' house.

At the end of the hallway there was a closed door, light leaking up from the floor from whatever lay on the other side. Frank paused outside it, his hand hovering near the handle, even as he told himself to turn back and go. Taking a breath, he reached out to take hold of it. He had come too far not to see this through.

He stepped into the next room, which proved to be the kitchen. There was a small circular table at the back, near a door that led to the rear entrance, around which sat two men. They looked up at him expectantly. Frank held up his hand, ready to apologize, already backing out the door.

"Good, you're here," a woman said.

Frank jumped. He hadn't noticed her standing in the corner,

looking over the stove. "Excuse me," he said apologetically, still backing away.

"Get in here. We've wasted enough time waiting for you already." This from the older of the two men at the table. His hair was sparse atop his head and close-cropped, while his jaw was covered in five days worth of greying beard. The other man was much younger, wide-eyed and clean shaven.

"I'm sorry," Frank said. "I think you've got the wrong guy. I just wandered in because I saw the door was open and wanted to make sure everything was alright."

The man snorted and rolled his eyes, while the woman by the stove laughed. "Please Frank," she said. "We don't believe that for a second. And we don't have time to waste. So let's get down to brass tacks, why don't we."

Frank nodded calmly, though his heart was pounding. How had she known his name? He sat opposite the man who had spoken and the woman joined them a moment later, carrying cups for all of them in one hand and a pot of coffee in the other. Frank held up his hand to decline the coffee, but the woman paid him no mind and poured him a cup.

He sighed. "Look," he started to say, but the old man shot him a glare.

"Go ahead Joe," the woman said. "Now that we're all here." She looked over at Frank.

Joe nodded. "Now listen up, I'm not going to repeat myself. We're not getting ourselves into another jackpot because we're careless. Ruthie, you've got the wheel. You know what to do, we've got no worries there." Here he looked across the table from Frank to the other man, as if to say that the problem, if there was one, lay with them.

"You two handle the customers and the tellers. Line them up against the wall. Make sure nobody tries to be the hero. Clear?"

"You got the wrong guy," Frank said, holding up his hands. "I been in some shit before, but whatever you're up to, I'm not signing up for it."

"Then why the hell are you here?" Joe said, leaning across the table, a challenge in his voice.

Frank was about to explain again, when he caught the eye of the other man, who shook his head in warning. He closed his mouth and looked at Joe, waiting for him to continue.

"Good. Don't get yellow on us now," Joe said with a sneer. "Now let's go over everything step by step."

He went through everything in detail. The entrance. The number of tellers. The number of guards. What they were to do, every step of the way. When he was done, he clapped his hands on the table authoritatively and announced, "I've gotta take a piss." He left the room and Ruthie got up and collected everyone's coffee cups, frowning at Frank's untouched one.

When she was over by the sink, running water, Frank leaned across the table and said in a low voice, "You know what the hell is going on here?"

The man shrugged. "You heard him."

"Oh, I get that," Frank said. "We're going to rob a bank. What I want to know is why the hell I'm being involved in this? Because I'm not who they think I am. I mean, I've not always been on the right side of the law, but I've never done anything like that. And I don't intend to start now."

The man looked at him with faintest of smiles. "You walked into the house didn't you?"

"Because the door was open. Because I thought something might be going on."

The man shrugged again. "Something is. You're here now. No getting out."

Frank laughed. "Oh, I'm leaving, make no mistake. I'm not getting stuck in this mess. Did you hear him? He didn't even mention the cameras, or the buzzer for the police. We're walking into a disaster. I'll be leaving in just a second."

The man shook his head. He spoke with a weary voice, sounding older than his years. "I think you'll find that's impossible. And forget about the cameras and all that other shit. That's not what you should be worried about."

"What do you mean?" Frank demanded. "What should I be worried about?"

The man smiled again, though there was no pleasure in it. His eyes were hollow, as if it had been weeks since he slept. "I walked in through that door, just like you. Sat at this table, just like you. Had the same damn conversation, near enough. And I'm still here. Every night we go and do the job, Ruthie, Joe and I. And whoever else walks through that door. Something always goes wrong. Sometimes someone dies. Maybe this time it'll be you. Or maybe it will finally be me. I hope so. I hope so."

Frank sat back in his chair. He wanted to argue with the man, but something in his expression told him it would be pointless. Any suggestion he could come up with for how to escape he, or the others with him, had already tried.

"How long have you been in here?"

The man held out his hands. "Who can say. It's all been one long night and day."

Joe came back from the other room, slipping on his coat. "You boys ready? Ruthie? Let's get on the road."

He walked out the backdoor and the man and Ruthie got up and followed behind. Frank looked around the room, as though trying to find a means to flee. There was none. He noted the old stove, the refrigerator that looked as though it had been put in when the house had been built, and everything else that seemed as though it had been kept in place for decades. It all told the same story. He got up and followed the others out the door.

LOST COORDINATES

The first call came that afternoon as Mary finally settled down to get some work done on her computer.

"Give me my fucking phone back cunt," the voice on other end of the call said. The man was more than angry, he sounded unhinged.

Mary was left disturbed and, after taking a moment to gather herself, she called the police. The officer listened sympathetically and took down a report, promising to follow up that week.

Not more than an hour later there was a knock at the door. When Mary got up from her computer she saw two police officers standing outside. *That was quick,* she thought, assuming they were following up on her earlier call.

"Ma'am, may we come in," the first officer, an unsmiling woman said. "We have a report that there is stolen property located here and we'd like to look around."

Mary blinked, a tiny ping of doubt echoing through her thoughts. "That's crazy. Do you have warrant?"

"We were hoping you would cooperate with us," the second officer said, offering a placating smile.

"I will. When you have a warrant. I can assure you, I haven't stolen anything. You're the second ones to accuse me of that today. The other one I had to report to the police."

Both officers frowned and glanced at each other. "When did this happen?" the woman said.

"About an hour ago," Mary said, and explained the phone call.

Neither officer had anything to say to her story. They thanked her for her time and retreated to their squad car, parked in front of the house. There they spent some time on the radio and their computers as Mary watched, glancing from time to time at the house. After half an hour they left and Mary finally allowed herself to relax, though she was still left unsettled. What was going on?

There were more calls that evening, with people demanding the return of their phones, computers, and other manner of electronica. The conversations all went much the same way, with Mary insisting she knew nothing of the lost gadgets, and the aggrieved owners growing angrier and angrier with their insistence that there could be no doubt as to the location of the devices. Tracking through various Find Me services and apps all pointed them to her address as the location for the lost items. The callers were, to judge by their phone numbers, spread across the region and even the state.

"GPS doesn't lie," as one of the callers said.

But, in this case, it had to be. It was simply impossible for Mary to have been responsible for dozens of thefts in the last two days, when she had left the house only once to refill a prescription at a drug store down the street.

Dutifully, after each call, she phoned the officer she had first spoken to and notified him of the complaint she had received. At his recommendation, she also contacted the phone company and the various Find Me services to let them know that there had to be some error in their tracking systems, that not all these devices could be located at her house. Everyone she spoke to was sympathetic, but ultimately unhelpful, with a hint of suspicion in their voices that began to wear at Mary.

The tracking systems appeared to be functioning as they should and there was no apparent explanation for why all these strangers should be seeing their devices located in her home. Except for the obvious. Her denials began to sound more and more desperate, even to her ears. Eventually, she had to turn off her phone and force herself to go to bed and sleep. Her dreams were filled with faceless voices accusing her of unspeakable acts, which she was forever unable to deny.

She awoke the next morning to an inbox full of irate voicemails. For the moment she decided to ignore them, setting about making coffee and some breakfast. There were two more calls as she did that, both of which she let go to voicemail. It was hard, in the face of this unending torrent of accusations, to continue to believe in her innocence. Even though she knew with certainty she had not taken anything. That it was impossible that she could have stolen all of them, given the volume of calls she was receiving. Never mind the fact that none of the devices were actually here.

And yet, more and more doubt began to slip into her mind. There was a glitch in the systems, that much seemed obvious. It was to her, at least. But not to anyone else, and her own certainty began to crumble.

The calls gave her no respite and she began to despair ever being free of them. They continued throughout the day and into the evening. She stopped answering her phone. Stopped reporting them to the police or the Find Me services. It all seemed so pointless. She turned off her phone and stared at her laptop screen, gone black from inactivity.

It was almost a relief when the police raided her house that evening. There was a knock at the door first. She had only just roused herself from her stupor to answer it when she heard glass breaking at the back of the house and the door being knocked down. Shouts followed, the incoherent code of command and response. Before she realized what was happening, Mary had been forced to the floor and cuffed, weapons trained at her head. She closed her eyes, willing this nightmare to disappear.

There was a shout, from what sounded like the basement. "Holy shit. Look at this."

A flurry of movement followed, all of which Mary could not track. She remained pressed to the ground, with her eyes closed. Eventually she heard the voice of, what she took to be, the commanding officer, the woman who had stood on her steps the day before. "Bag and tag it all. Read her her rights."

The whole world seemed to disappear in that moment and the next thing Mary recalled was sitting in the interrogation room in the precinct downtown. The woman and her partner were sitting across from her, staring with grim faces. Mary could not recall either of their names. They were asking her questions. They had been asking them for some time, but Mary could not recall them all, or for how long they had been here. Time had blurred together and vanished somehow. Even now, reality seemed tenuous, and she was hesitant to do anything for fear of sending it spiraling away from her grasp.

"Not answering us isn't going to do you any good," the woman said. It felt like this was not the first time she had said the words. "We found twenty five phones that match those that were reported stolen. And thirty other devices. How did those end up in your basement?"

They weren't there. They couldn't have been. This was all a terrible mistake. That was what Mary had wanted to say, but she couldn't find the words. They wouldn't believe her anyway.

"There must be some reason, right? Help us understand." The other officer gave her a lying smile. Mary blinked.

"What I don't understand is how you could find the time to steal all these phones. I don't think you could've done it alone. Who was working with you? What was the end game here?"

Mary shook her head helplessly.

"We can help you out. You just need to tell us who you were working for. That's who we want, right? What else were you into?"

Nothing, Mary wanted to say, but didn't. She knew she should be asking for a lawyer. Denying everything. But she couldn't. It wasn't in her too.

"How did you do it Mary? And why?" Help us understand."

Mary looked from face to face, her whole body seeming to vibrate with anguish, and she began to tell them.

THE FACE OF THE EMPRESS

Blan was known to all in Agash for the sweet confection of fruit, candy and shaved ice he sold, called h'al-h'al. He worked at stall near the market where traders would pass by. Agash lay on one of the salt roads, so merchants and strangers were the norm. But Blan had never seen someone like the woman who appeared at his stall one afternoon.

It was a particularly hot day and her face was streaked with dust from the road. She purchased a cup of h'al-h'al from Blan, paying with an old coin. In studying it, Blan did not recognize the empress stamped upon it.

"How much is this in standard? I don't know what change to give you."

The woman waved him away. "No matter. I'll have no need for it soon enough." She spoke with an odd accent, a lilt that Blan was certain he had never heard before. Her eyes and her dress were strange as well, even by the standards of Agash, where it was said the known worlds passed by. It was an old phrase, and no longer true, for there was only one world now.

"I hope you're not in any trouble." Blan said, though he didn't know why. He knew better than to involve himself in the lives of strangers. Doing so led to problems, and those he could not afford.

She gave him an odd smile. "We're all of us in trouble, more or less. Some of us just realize it better than others."

Blan gave a wary shrug. "I guess. You like it?"

"Delicious," she said, still smiling, and asked for his name. He

127

told her, after a moment's hesitation. "I will see you soon, Blan of Agash," she said, and took her leave.

Everyone knew there was not one world, but many. It was the ways between them that were lost. Forgotten by the slow entropy of time, or—some said—hidden by those who wanted the power kept for themselves. Regardless, the gates remained closed and concealed. Even the maps and ancient texts that referenced them, provided no illumination on their location. They led to meadows and cliffs, lost villages where once people had lived, and the middle of coursing rivers.

The world had changed in the course of millennia, and with it the location of the gates, that much seemed evident, though how that could be possible no one was certain. Most accepted this as the lot of the fallen times in which they lived. There were far more important matters to concern them. Empires and Republics that rose and fell. Plagues and pestilences. Crops that flourished and failed.

Blan knew about the known worlds, but gave them no thought. They were like the strangers who came to Agash and promised him this and that, only to disappear without a word. He remained, going about his days as always.

That night, as he returned to the quarters he shared with his parents, the woman was waiting for him near the door. He was tired, already thinking of his bed, and did not see her as she emerged from the shadows.

"Blan of Agash," she said. "How was your day?"

He froze, unsure how to respond and deeply unsettled by both her question and her appearance here. "How did you know where I lived?"

"Ask a few questions and you will receive answers in this town. Especially if you have strange coins no one knows the value of."

Blan thought of his own coin. "Are they worthless?"

"Priceless. You will not find another like it in the known worlds."

Blan frowned. "What do you want?"

The woman appeared to be in no hurry. She looked up at the sky, studying the various stars. "They're all so dim here. It's strange. I hadn't thought they'd be different."

Blan took a step toward the door, feeling annoyed now, and not wanting to waste anymore time with this woman. "You're going to tell me you're from the other known worlds. That's impossible. Everybody knows."

"I am," she said, her voice sounding loud in the quiet of the street.

"Do you know how many madmen come through Agash claiming this and that. None of what they say is true. Neither is this. Go away and leave me alone. I have to be up early tomorrow."

"I am a madwoman, of that there's no doubt. But it's also true that I came from another world." Her manner changed. She was abrupt and desperate.

Blan narrowed his eyes. "And why should I believe you?"

"It doesn't matter whether you do or not. I had thought." Here she paused, looking at the sky again. "It's too bad I don't have more time. I'd hoped I would. And so you see, it doesn't matter whether you believe me or not. You'll know the truth soon enough."

"I see," Blan said, feeling confused, which along with his exhaustion made him angry. "Can I find out the truth tomorrow, when I've had a night's sleep? You can come find me at my stand and you can buy another h'al-h'al with one of your fine coins and tell me all about the known worlds."

The woman smiled. She seemed older than he remembered, but perhaps it was just the darkness of the night shadowing her face. "This is the last time we shall ever chance to meet Blan of Agash. Keep that coin close. Whatever happens, don't let anyone else have it. It will see you through the rest of your days. That I guarantee."

"I will. I promise," Blan said, more to end the conversation than out of any real intent on his part. "Now I must go to bed. I wish you good luck in your journeys."

"And I wish you more luck in yours than I've had in mine."

Blan was about to say that he was not journeying anywhere—poor foodsellers like him did not go on journeys—but she had already turned to go and he hurried in to bed.

The following day, as Blan sat under the awning of his stall to hide from the afternoon sun, two officials approached, along with a third man who was dressed as oddly as the woman had been. Behind them, two servants dragged a wagon along. Blan leapt to his feet, ready to prepare h'al-h'al for all, but the officials waved at him to stop. "We have questions for you," the first said.

"Do you recognize this woman?" the second said, gesturing to the wagon.

He went over to peer over its side and saw the woman lying there, her eyes closed. Blan looked at the two officials and nodded. They in turn looked to the stranger and nodded, gesturing to him to proceed. He did, stepping forward to study Blan with his hard eyes.

"I understand the woman came to your stand. What did she say to you?" the man said, his voice as hard edged as his eyes.

Blan quivered, but did not look away. "Nothing. She bought some h'al-h'al. She liked it."

"And that was the last you saw her?"

Blan hesitated, remembering her words to him last night. "No," he said. "I saw her going home last night. She said she was going on a journey and I wouldn't see her again."

The stranger frowned. "There was nothing else?"

Blan shrugged. "She said the sky seemed different here. I didn't know what to think of that."

"Indeed," the man said. He smiled and Blan had to smother the shudder of horror her felt at the sight of it. The stranger did not appear to notice. He turned away, about to say something to the officials, when he stopped and turned back to Blan. "What did she pay you with?"

Blan was taken aback. "A coin, sir."

"Obviously. What coin? I would like to see it."

Blan blinked, recalling the woman's words to him the night before. Keep it close. It seemed sensible advice. He fished into his pocket and pulled out one of the tarnished crowns a trader from Nar had given him that morning.

"It was something like this," he said, handing it over.

The man looked at it. "You are certain this is the coin."

Blan gave an elaborate shrug. "One coin is much like the other."

The stranger looked at him, his lips curling into a snarl, and he threw the coin away in disgust. He strode away, the officials scurrying behind him. Blan watched them go, fingering the woman's coin in his pocket as he did. When the officials and the stranger were gone, he wandered over and to pick up the crown and sat down to await his next customer.

ALL THE TIME

The woman had close-cropped, dark hair in an unfamiliar style. But Dez rarely recognized styles, be they clothing, hair or make-up anymore. It was the marker of all the time that passed while he was in-ship. That was its own time, both faster and slower than the time for those outside it. He lived his days normally, as any other, and on these worlds decades, sometimes even centuries passed.

So much changed that he often experienced a sense of vertigo when he emerged to see what there was of the universe. What did not change, what was constant as the stars themselves, was the urge. It was quiet in-ship, biding its time, knowing that its moment would come. But once he stepped onto these teeming planets, ripe with possibility, it could not be denied.

The woman did not notice him slipping into the flow of the crowd to follow her down the street. This city had streets, open to the elements, as Dez's own home had. He could remember so little specific about it now. Somehow in-ship had become his default environment, what he associated normal with. Off it, the assault of color and noise, the press of people, the endless space extending on through vast constructions, was all foreign and other.

Most of those who went in-ship did so on one way voyages. They had their reasons. Others, a select few, such as Dez, lived in-ship, going from port to port, letting the centuries drift past. They would grow old in-ship and die there, a thousand years or more after their birth. It was a kind of immortality, though a meager .

And a sequestered one, for most could not stomach more than

brief visits while in port to the worlds and what they held. Some drink and some companionship, though even those basic needs could become complicated by several centuries of cultural detritus, were all they were looking for. Most of his shipmates avoided it, staying aboard and interacting only with those on the docks, where they were treated as a kind of bizarre nobility. Dez always availed himself of the opportunities to stretch his legs and see what there was to be seen. As claustrophobic and nauseous as it was, there were things he had to see to.

The woman stopped off to pick up some food, or at least that was what Dez surmised she was doing. The shop looked like what he had known as a grocery store, with brightly colored boxes lining endless shelves. He loitered outside the shop, enjoying watching the shifting crowd move around him.

Dez was so immersed in the crowd's movements that he almost missed when the woman emerged from the store and started down the street. She made her way to what Dez referred to as the air-train—he had ridden one on his way from the dock—and he was behind her when she got on. He stood near enough to get a taste of her scent, but not so near as to draw her attention. The car was crowded with people heading home from work and no one paid him any mind.

Nor did anyone pay any mind as he followed her into the vast complex that proved to be her apartment building. By its exterior, he would have guessed it was a manufacturing plant or something like that, and perhaps it once had been. He almost lost her again in the maze of corridors—the elevators, heading in every conceivable direction were utterly baffling. But he did not panic and, eventually, he came upon her trail again.

When the urge was upon him, the heat of it in his blood, his instincts were always true. That was why he was not at all surprised when he slipped into the tiny cubicle where she made her home, to find she was alone. It meant he could linger and take his time, which he always preferred. Like anything else, there were some he enjoyed more than others. Some that seemed rote, some that he regretted. But this one was special, the liquidity in her eyes, when she realized he was there, was breathtaking.

As he took the air-train back to the docks, he was overcome by a wistful kind of regret. Even one like this—where everything had gone as smoothy as he could imagine, and where the act itself had been glorious and overwhelming—could never compare to what was in his head. That was why, he was certain, the urge always returned. Someday he would craft that perfect act and he would be done. He could walk back into time.

But he never would, he knew. There was no perfect act. Nothing could quell the urge that swelled within him, like clockwork when the end of his in-ship spell ended.

He was back on ship before dawn broke. In all likelihood, he and his vessel would already be launched and on its way to its next destination before the body was even discovered. That was how he planned it, and except for a few clumsy attempts, how it normally went. He was a ghost in the system, flitting in and gone, out of time. Not even a suspect or considered.

Once he had returned to the planet he had been born without realizing it. The site of his first. Centuries had passed. People had lived and died and the woman—a striking thing with green eyes and freckles he could still picture—had long since been forgotten. Another case unsolved. The governments responsible for finding her killer had collapsed and been reborn a half dozen times or more since. Nothing remained of her but his memory of those final moments.

It was dark, the sky still filled with stars, including the one that he would be going to next, when he arrived at the ship. By the time he came to rest again, everyone on this world would be dead, and he would be somewhere else, following another woman.

THE CONTRAPTION

Jules Amostel had been tinkerer all his days, from his youth when his parents gave him a chemistry set to play with, through his time at university in the engineering department, where he was constantly toying with circuits in the lab or in his dorm room, and later as he found himself a job working for the city transit department. The first thing he did upon the purchase of a house, after marrying his longtime girlfriend, was to turn the unfinished basement into a lab space for the various projects he embarked on.

Jules had never been particularly social, and while he enjoyed going out and meeting with friends, and got on well with all his co-workers, he needed time to himself to do as he pleased and found it in the basement. His wife Ana was a patient woman and recognized it as a release of sorts from the stresses of day to day living. Every now and again she would notice him spending too much time alone down there and would remind him that he needed to spend time with her and his friends. She did not ask much about what he did there and he volunteered little, showing her the odd device he built, but they mostly confused her.

Soon they had children and their lives became busier still. Jules found time when he could for his work in the basement, though admittedly less now. It did not bother him, his daughters were far more intriguing than anything he might work on down below. As they grew into their teens and became more independent, he found he had more time that he could devote to his work and he returned to it with a renewed vigor. Sunday became his day dedicated to his devices and he would descend below after breakfast while Amy and his daughters entertained themselves.

Finally, after twenty five years of intermittent work, Jules finished what he had begun so long ago in his university dorm room. The individual devises that had so confused Amy were but a part of a much grander whole—a vast contraption—that, when he finally assembled it, took up much of the basement. It was capable of traversing time and space, perhaps even the fabric of the universe itself.

It was his life's work, his grand design, but for many weeks he did not engage the contraption, would not enter it. Fear stopped him short. What if he turned it on and he was sent somewhere or sometime and could not return? Worse, what if nothing happened at all? It was difficult to say which of those possibilities scared him most.

At last though, temptation and curiosity won out, and one Sunday morning he turned the various devices on and entered the contraption. It whirred and hissed, lights blinking, fans blowing and something like an engine growling. The hairs on his arms rose up and he felt a strange itch in the back of his throat. There was a whiff of smoke as well, which concerned him greatly. He had a vision of Amy and the kids smelling it and coming down to investigate before he managed to return. How would he explain what had happened? What if they interfered with the contraption?

Before he had time to worry any further about his family the contraption stopped, its engines slowing until the only sound was the fan cooling its motors. A new world, he thought to himself as he set his shoulders and stepped out of the device.

When he did he saw that he was still in his basement, which to all appearances was unchanged from the few minutes before when he had entered. Perhaps the contraption had malfunctioned. A quick check revealed no obvious problems. Everything had apparently functioned as it should have, yet here he was, exactly where he had left. He was still pondering what could have gone wrong when Amy called down to him. Reluctantly, he left the contraption and went upstairs.

"Where have you been all afternoon?" Amy said, as he came up to the foot of the stairs.

"In the basement working," he said, and was amazed to see that it was growing dark outside. Excitement gripped him. What had felt like only minutes to him had evidently been hours. The contraption had worked, the process just needed to be refined.

"On what?"

"The same thing I work on every Sunday," Jules said. He was surprised to see Amy looking oddly at him. Patricia, his youngest daughter, was at the kitchen table and she too was looking at him with a confused expression.

"I don't know what you're talking about dear," Amy said, her voice sounding strained. Patricia stood up from her chair and looked from face to face, as though expecting an eruption to occur.

"How can you not know what I'm talking about?" Jules said, the color going from his face, his stomach twisting at the thoughts that slipped through his mind. "I go down there every Sunday to work on my things. Do you think I'm just sitting there doing nothing? I've shown you what I worked on for god sakes."

"Dad," Patricia said, holding out a hand as though to calm and console him. Amy's face, he saw, was twisted with emotion. He thought he saw tears in her eyes.

Without another word he turned and went back down the stairs. He understood what had happened. The contraption had worked, he was in another universe. This one was just like his own, except that here he had not developed the contraption. What did the other Jules do? And where was he now?

As he descended, barely able to reign in his panic, he heard Amy tell Patricia not to follow him. Things were very different in this universe, he realized, in spite of appearances. He had to get back to his own. Hopefully there were no issues with the contraption and he could reverse the process that had brought him here. He could not be sure until he tried. He would have to careful the next time he used it, for it was obviously even more powerful than he had realized.

These thoughts clattered through his mind in such a rush that his brain felt as though it could not possibly hold them all. They all vanished as he reached the bottom of the stairs and turned round the corner to where his workshop was, where the contraption sat, only to see an empty unfinished basement and nothing more.

A LIGHT

It began sometime after Beata put on her coat—the long winter one that came down to her thighs and clung to her form in a way she liked—and left her office. She had just left the building and was on her way, walking with purpose, her boot heels clicking in that pleasant rhythm she enjoyed. The day was cool but pleasant, with no breeze bringing an extra chill. A skiff of snow had fallen during the night and the way it caught the light made the day seem vibrant and alive.

Beata adjusted her purse on her shoulder and halted mid-stride. She nearly fell over so abrupt was her stop. Someone brushed by her, muttering and shooting her a quick glare. Her hands were tingling as though she had absorbed some electricity. Even her hair felt as though it were rising off her head from a static charge. She reached out to touch her curls, but everything felt in place.

When she was certain that everything was in its right place and the effects of the charge—or whatever it had been—had passed, Beata started forward again. Only to stop a moment later. She could no longer recall what she had been doing, or where she had been going. That she had left the office to go somewhere was clear. A glance at her watch showed that it was two in the afternoon, too early for her to be leaving work. So it was an errand.

She looked around and saw that she was heading down the street away from where she normally parked her car and assumed that she was on her way to the nearby strip mall. What she had to do there she still didn't know, but she started forward anyway,

137

certain that it would come to her eventually. Instead, as she came to the end of the block, she saw her car parked across the street. She stopped again and stared at it, utterly mystified.

Beata pulled out her keys to press the unlock button just to be sure it was her vehicle. The lights flashed and she could hear the locks click open. She had no memory of parking it here, no sense of why she would have when she had her own parking stall on the other side of her office building. It was strange. Disturbing even. What else had she forgotten?

She cast her mind back over her day and there were suspicious gaps throughout. She could remember her breakfast, but not the drive into work. There had been coffee with Anna Lisse, followed by some emails. Other than that, the details of her morning were beyond her grasp. She had been in her office she felt certain, but could not recall any of the documents she had worked on. There had been an appointment over lunch, but she could no longer remember what it had been. Had she had to drive? And been forced to park here? Was that what she was doing now, going to collect her car?

Her thoughts seemed to be coming all at once, question after question emerging from the depths. All with no answers. She walked unsteadily over to the car and got in, holding the keys in her hand, not yet willing to start it. When she finally did she drove back to her parking spot and returned upstairs to the office.

"Wow. That was quick," Anna Lisse said, as Beata walked past her desk.

"I couldn't remember why I left in the first place," Beata said, giving a shake of her head. "Oldzheimers I guess."

Anna Lisse laughed. "You didn't tell me actually. Just said you needed to go home. I thought you'd forgotten a file."

"I don't think so," Beata said.

"It'll come back to you eventually."

Beata nodded, but she felt none of Anna Lisse's confidence. She returned to her office and sat down to look at her computer screen. It was black, but she made no move to turn it back on or log in, lost in its blank void. The tingling returned to her fingers, rising up her arms to her shoulders. She let out a cry, almost a moan. Not in pleasure and not in pain.

"Are you okay?" Anna Lisse called from the other room.

Beata did not respond. The words would not come to her. Her

consciousness seemed to have slipped into the background, where her thoughts still spun feverishly, to no effect. The rest of her being was filled with the ever-expanding void of her computer screen. Only it wasn't a void: the universe in its entirety was there, blossoming before her very eyes. Her whole body was suffused with tremors, which she gradually came to realize matched the rhythm of particles vibrating around her.

The pitch of the universe was c-sharp. The thought came forth and vanished as she saw more and more. Galaxies beyond number. Stars, black holes, planets. Things beyond her imagining. It was all there, all in a moment.

Anna Lisse had entered the room. She was calling Beata's name, her voice frantic. Beata did not respond. The moment was too powerful. She was under its sway.

"It's some kind of seizure. I don't know. Send an ambulance."

Time had expanded, so that she could see all of it, from the beginning to end. Both were dark and without form. And then there was a light.

Beata turned to Anna Lisse and smiled.

THE DOOR

No one could recall when last the door had been opened. Lifetimes, some said. Centuries, claimed others. There were those in fact who stated, with an air of quiet authority, that it never had been, that it had always remained closed. All agreed that no one alive had opened the door, or had known of anyone who had. All they knew was the stories their parents told, which their parents had told them, back through time where the collective memory became misted and cloudy.

Philosophers would often argue about the door, launching into great disquisitions on their theories surrounding why the door had or had not to have been opened. There were even those who said that the door should be opened, for stories were nothing more than stories, and the true nature of the door could only be discerned by seeing what lay behind it. None of them, of course, volunteered to bear witness to what was beyond that terrible threshold, even those who professed to believe that nothing was there to be found.

Most, though, did not give in to such foolish and idle thinking. The stories told were so uniformly terrible, and all so similar, that there simply had to be some truth to what was said. It could not be otherwise, no matter what some radical thinkers might claim. Most importantly, no one wanted to be the one to discover they were in fact true, for the horrors described were so awful there could be no encountering them without a life being changed irrevocably.

Though no one would dare to so much as approach the door,

to say nothing of putting a hand upon the handle, or even pretending to turn it, there came a time when the leading citizens of the day determined that someone needed to be set to watch it, to ensure that no one made the mistake of opening it. Two men were set to the task, both of them considered to be honest and upstanding, the finest among them. One took the daylight hours and one took the night.

It was a long and lonely job for both, with most days passing without event. Though their jobs were hardly strenuous physically, both men were left exhausted by the end of each shift, their constant vigilance and the absence of any activity weighing heavily upon their minds. Both considering quitting and yet both persisted, knowing how important what they were doing was. If one misguided youth or extremist philosopher should take it into their head to do the unthinkable, someone needed to be there to stop them.

Still, as the days stretched into weeks and then months and finally years, and no one came near them as they kept their vigil, let alone making any attempt to open the door, a change gradually took hold in both of them. Instead of becoming complacent in their duties, as might be expected, they redoubled their efforts. No one could question the importance of their task, or the awful nature of the threat the door represented, least of all them.

A strange logic took hold in their minds. They came to believe that, because they were standing vigil, someone must be attempting to open the door. If they could find no evidence of such attempts, then it only meant they were unable to find it through the means available to them. They needed to look deeper into everything, to trust nothing, not even their own senses. Sinister powers were obviously at work.

Each man brought in necromancers and alchemists, philosophers and academicians, to study the matter. None of them could find any evidence of malfeasance. None could even suggest how such a thing could be done without the two men noticing. If they were both there on duty at all times—and both men were unimpeachable, so there could be no doubt—then all agreed it simply could not be done. The men would notice somehow. They would see the attempt.

This satisfied neither man and each separately came to the same realization. The only people who were unwatched around the door were they themselves. Each knew they had not allowed temptation to steal into their hearts, but what of their counterpart? Could he be trusted?

They each decided the other could not, and they each began to maintain a constant vigil, secreting themselves near the door while the other was on duty. Such a task proved impossible, for they could not hope to stay awake the entire day, and when, inevitably, they fell asleep while observing the other, they became convinced that it was during these moments the other must have opened the door and passed through.

After some weeks of their mutual and unbeknownst observation of each other, they each reached the same, inevitable conclusion. The only way to catch the other was to do so in the act. And the only way to do so was to enter the door themselves and wait within. It was a terrible risk to take, but both concluded it was the only acceptable solution.

They knew each other's habits so well by then that it was an easy thing to do. The man set to watch the day, knowing that the night watchman's habit was to first walk a wide perimeter around the door when he started his shift, greeted the man warmly at day's end and waited until the other had set upon his walk. As soon as the man's back was turned, he reached out and grasped the door handle, turned and slipped within, closing it quietly behind him.

When the night watchman returned from his route and saw that the day watchman was gone he thought only that he could put his own plan into action. He intended to go through the door sometime before dawn, reasoning that his absence in the morning would be enough to tempt the other into going within as well, to make certain that his dark secrets were not being discovered. As the first light of day approached, the shadows gradually giving way, he did just that.

It was late in the afternoon when someone passing near the door happened to notice the day watchman was not on duty. She rushed to notify the citizenry and they immediately made their way to rouse the nightwatchman, only to discover that he too had disappeared. A search was called and the entire populace scoured every block, every nook and every cranny, every sewer and every roof, but no sign of either man was ever found.

THE TRADES

THE WARDER

Xan the Warder stared at the newcomer with a skeptical eye. The man was a sorcerer of some kind, to judge by his robes. Xan knew little of magic, but enough to know that its users were not to be trusted. They were fiends, as likely to summon some demon from the depths of the many earths as to cast a curing spell and mend a broken leg. She had heard tell of a man, desperate in his affections for a woman, who had begged a wizard for a love potion, only to find himself short six coins of the realm and madly in love with a toad.

"What brings you this way, stranger?" Xan said. She swept the cloak back from her shoulders and let her hand rest upon her sword. A message of sorts.

The newcomers gaze followed the movement of her hand and a small grin touched his lips. "I've heard the air in these parts is restorative."

"If you can restore something that's been froze solid with your magic, then perhaps it might be," Xan said, looking out over the frigid wastes that extended in all directions before her.

The newcomer laughed, his breath clouding the air. "My name is Ves. You are?"

"The Warder," Xan said, refusing to be enticed by his friendliness. The wind swirled around them and the sorcerer shivered.

"Where's the prison?" Ves said.

"Do you think I'm a fool?"

Ves laughed again. "I suppose not. It is a rather remote clime for a prison, wouldn't you agree?"

Xan did not reply, staring hard at the sorcerer.

Ves shrugged, as if he could not understand her reluctance to talk. "Come now, Warder. Surely you must get bored being here, all alone in the cold? I'm only asking for a moment of your time."

Xan rolled her eyes. "No one comes here to pass the time. I'm not much for conversation. Get to the point." She moved her hand to the pommel of her sword.

"Easy now," Ves said, holding up his hands. "Don't you think you should be careful? You don't know what kind of sorcerer I am."

"It doesn't matter," Xan said, her voice sounding of death.

Ves smiled. "If you say so. You needn't worry about me anyway, Warder. I'm just here to meet someone."

Xan had to resist a laugh. "I doubt there is someone else in the realm foolish enough to wander out onto this wasteland for a chat."

"But there is," Ves said, gesturing with his hand as if to point out the person.

Xan followed the movement of his hand and the world went black.

She blinked, worried for a moment that the sorcerer had put a sleeping spell upon her. But it was just that the light had gone from the sky, which, now that she thought about it, was considerably more concerning than a mere sleep spell. The light returned a moment later, the vast wasteland of ice, snow and rock, appearing again before her.

The sorcerer, however, was gone.

She could almost swear she heard his laughter from somewhere behind her. That, she knew, was impossible. Though she dearly wanted to turn around to confirm that, she resisted, her eyes alight to any movements before her. She fingered the pommel of her sword, but did not draw it. Now was not the time to panic.

Her patience paid off as the air before her shimmered, a glare of light coming forth, refracting off the snow, and the sorcerer emerged with a kind of shrug, as if to say he was sorry, but he had to try.

"Ah well," he said, looking mildly embarrassed. "I don't

suppose you would believe I was just over that hill looking for my friend."

"I would not," Xan said.

"Perhaps we can come to some sort of understanding." Ves reached into his robes, as if searching for his purse.

Xan pulled her sword, baring an inch or two of steel, but keeping the rest within her scabbard. "We cannot."

"I see," Ves said, nodding. "Well, it appears I've wasted my time here."

"And mine," Xan said.

"Apologies Warder, but—"

"Do not waste anymore," Xan said, raising a hand to forestall him. "My patience is at an end."

Ves nodded again, his eyes downcast. "I see. I understand entirely. It must be so hectic here, watching the wastes. Hard to find the time for anything really. Has anyone told you that you look lovely in the frost?"

"Be gone." The frigid air seemed to crack and groan around them at her words.

Ves winced, looking behind him, as if he expected an avalanche to sweep him away. "Yes, of course. And I will, certainly. But before I do, you must admit that you get lonely out here. A solitary sentinel against the scoundrels of the world."

Xan resisted a sigh. "Whether I get lonely is no concern of yours. But you needn't worry about me, I have enough scoundrels to deal with."

"But do any of them warm your heart?"

"My heart needs no warming," Xan said, thinking of the man in love with a frog. If she was not mindful, she might end up lusting after a raven, or an outcropping of rocks, or whatever else in this vast empty land the sorcerer laid his eyes upon.

"But it's so cold and so lonely here. Surely you must long for a moment of surrender?" Ves looked hopeful, as if that surrender might come with him.

Xan rolled her eyes. "Honoring my duty is warmth enough, I can assure you."

She tapped at her exposed sword with a finger indicating that his time was up. The sorcerer nodded, ducking his head a little, as if he realized he could delay no more. He started to turn away, before stopping, his eyes brightening, as if something had just occurred to him.

"Could I entreat you with a bribe?"

"What sort of bribe?"

The sorcerer considered the question, clearly suspecting some sort of trick. "I know many spells that might be useful. Love spells, hate spells, killing spells, and spells of transmutation. That is only a selection. I'm sure I have one that would meet your needs."

Xan considered this a moment. "Do you have a spell that can transport a person somewhere?"

"Yes," Ves said eagerly. "The only question is where. To a warmer clime perhaps?"

"That would be agreeable," Xan said. "Now, what would you have me do?"

"There is a certain prisoner held here." He gestured behind Xan, though that was not where the prison was concealed. "A Yon."

"I know the knave."

"He is only here due to a slight misunderstanding between him and the magistrate. Some matter involving the Duke's wife. I won't bore you with the particulars. If we are agreed, then you can set him free and I will cast the spell."

"We are agreed," Xan said. She extended a hand and they shook upon their agreement.

"Excellent," Ves said, rubbing his hands together in delight. "Now, tell me where you would like me to send you."

"It is not I who I wish to send away," Xan said.

Ves looked at her blankly.

"I want you to transport yourself away. Somewhere across the far seas will be acceptable."

"But our agreement," Ves sputtered.

"I will honor it," Xan said in a calm voice. "The scoundrel Yon will be released, as soon as you transport yourself away."

"But what good is that? If he is here alone, how can he hope to make his escape?"

"He cannot," Xan said. "He will be arrested for attempted escape. There will, of course, be some punishment incurred for that."

Ves looked at her, a sour expression on his face. "You are a trickster, Warder."

Xan shrugged. "We have an agreement. We shook before the

gods. I expect you to honor it. If you don't, I can arrest you and place you here."

The sorcerer gave a bitter shake of his head and vanished, the air flashing in the place where he had stood. Xan smiled and pulled her cloak tighter around her shoulders.

D.B.

D.B. stepped up to the bar. "Bourbon and water," he said, with a nod to the bartender.

"Sure. Got a particular flavor?" the bartender said.

D.B. shook his head and the bartender busied himself with a bottle of his cheapest. His sleeves were rolled up to this elbow and his arms were lined with tattoos. D.B. found himself staring at them.

"You like the ink?" the bartender asked as he passed the bourbon over.

D.B. shook his head. "Never much cared for it."

"No?" the bartender said with a smile. "Guess not many folks your age have them."

"You'd be surprised. I was in the navy. Lot of the boys had them then. I never did. And it was a good thing. Easy way for people to remember you."

"Some of us want to be remembered," the bartender said.

"Sure," D.B. said. "Some do. Some don't."

By his tone he made it plain which he preferred. The bartender looked as though he were about to reply but another customer, a young woman with large glasses, entered and he went to her. D.B. took a sip of his bourbon and cast about the room with a studied eye, noting the exits and the few people present. An old habit, one he did not intend to lose.

There were no more than a half dozen people in the place at this hour—a grubby little bar with pretensions to being hip, that didn't quite manage it. Most of them were young—D.B. had a half-century on all of them, he would guess—and absorbed in the heat of their lives. Only the bartender paid him any mind, with, what seemed to D.B., a genuine curiosity as to why an old man was having a bourbon in his establishment at two in the afternoon.

When D.B. was finished his first bourbon the bartender made his way over. "Care for another?"

"Sure. I got the time." He could feel a twinge of his old accent coming back into his voice as he spoke. It was always there, hidden, but visible. Something he had to watch for.

"Great. Big plans for the rest of the day?"

"Can't say as I do. I'm done with big plans."

The bartender chuckled. "They never work out, do they?"

D.B shrugged. "Sometimes they do. It's always harder than you think, though. And then you wonder if it was all worth it."

The bartender gave a helpless shrug and went to refill a pint for the girl with the glasses. D.B. took a sip of the bourbon and looked her over. A cute thing, he had to admit, though he didn't like the glasses. She reminded him of someone, though he couldn't say who. Someone from another life, most likely.

Moments like this, these brief little interludes he allowed himself, were the only companionship he had. Friends were risky, lovers even more so. What he did—what he had done—required a discipline that had to adhered to absolutely. There could be no allowances made, no exceptions. It was an iron rule. That discipline, and the patience to wait, to not give in to haste or impetuousness. No long term ties, nothing that he couldn't walk away from without a second thought. These were the things that had kept him free, alive, and able to live out his reward.

"What brings you here?" the bartender said, coming back over to talk to him.

D.B. frowned. The kid was curious, which meant he would remember this old man he was talking to, at least for a time. He regretted coming in here. This was supposed to be a minor celebration—a private one—of his return.

"Just visiting some old haunts," D.B. said.

"Oh yeah. You been here before?"

D.B. shook his head. "Nah. Lived in Tacoma for a few years, you know. I'm just passing through and thought I'd see the old neighborhoods. Catch up with some folks."

The bartender nodded and went to fix a gin and tonic. D.B. grimaced as he walked away. Getting chatty in his old age. There was no need to be going and telling him all that. It was too near the truth. Mistakes added up, and they led to others.

Still, he had to admit, he was probably being overcautious. It had been twenty years since he'd last set foot in Tacoma. That had been after a long, solitary walk through the forest in winter. He'd nearly died those two nights, nearly died coming off the plane. That had been risky, but a risk he'd needed to take. And there had been mistakes then as well.

It had taken some time to disappear, but he'd done so. Everything had been exactingly planned and carried out to the letter. Dozens of suspects had been named, and presumably investigated, but they'd never come near to finding him. They were always looking in the wrong places, for someone who had a history of that sort of thing. He had none, at least nothing they would know of.

His time had been spent planning, planning and waiting for the right moment to set everything in motion. Once it had started, he'd just gone through with everything and hoped that his luck would hold. When it did, he waited again. First for the money to be cleaned and then for enough time to pass that he wouldn't be noticed.

This had always been the plan, and now that it was at an end he felt an odd sense of emptiness. What had been the point of it all? The plan had defined everything and now it was through and he was left with nothing to do. A man approaching his sixties, the best of his life behind him, and he had to start over. He felt a twinge of regret and pushed it aside with the last sip of his bourbon. No time to be worrying about that now. He'd find a new plan, a new set of rules. That would be nice.

He shook his head as the bartender came over to offer him another bourbon, slipping some money on the counter of the bar, and headed to the bathroom. It reeked of piss and urinal cakes, everything looking as though it were barely holding together, graffiti tagged on every wall. As he worked his zipper open, he heard the door behind him swing open, squeaking as it did.

"Old man."

It was a woman who spoke and when he turned around he saw the girl with big glasses standing there. She had a small pistol in her hand and was screwing on a silencer. He stared at her open mouthed, his hands still at his open fly.

"You recognize me old man?" She spoke in a clipped tone, with the barest hint of an accent.

She was familiar. D.B. struggled to remember how he knew her. "You were in the casino in Vegas," he said at last.

"I was there long before that. I've been on your trail for a long time D.B. Do you know why?"

He shook his head. "If it's the money you want—"

"It isn't. You never had time to look at me. You were always looking at that damn money. Even before it was there."

With those words, D.B. did recognize her. His eyes widened. She raised the gun and shot him, twice, near the heart. He fell to the bathroom floor with a soft groan, thinking that it had never occurred to him. Never occurred to him at all. He was staring up as she came to stand over him and put a bullet in his head, but he already couldn't see.

THE COOLING BOARD

The storm that swept through Dagar that night as most of the city slumbered, left in its wake a tangled forest of broken branches and fallen trees, along with remnants of shacks and huts cast asunder. As the clean up began in neighborhood after neighborhood, the body of a young man was discovered in amongst the detritus on the outskirts of Gasnon, one of the less reputable areas of the city. The constabulary was summoned and, after a quick survey of the scene, they took the body to the central mortuary.

There the Chief Magistrate viewed the body and noted in the records that the death had been the result of the storm. No one in the neighborhood where the body was discovered had known the youth—hardly strange, given the district's attraction to those desperate souls who flocked to Dagar with no coin hoping to resurrect their fortunes. The Chief Magistrate noted that, by his color, the youth was a Mannurary and had the local Caciques brought to the mortuary to see if they could identify him. They dutifully put on their finest suits and came to look upon the body, all of them declaring they had never laid eyes on the man.

The Chief Magistrate thanked the elders for their time and had them promise to inform him if they received word that the youth had family who were missing him. He did not expect them to, for there were so many people, Mannurary or otherwise, who came to Dagar, alone and in search of a better life, only to end up on the streets, destitute and broken. They waited a day at the mortuary for someone to come forward to claim the body, and when no claimant materialized, the chief magistrate ordered it be laid upon a cooling board with ice beneath it and set out in the public room.

There were three other bodies on display when the Mannurary youth was set out for viewing, and two more joined him the next day. These were a, not unusual, assortment of unfortunates: a harlot beaten to death by her keeper; an old man,who, having lost one of his legs some years before , subsisted on the streets, relying on the kindness of passersby; a priest who had become overly drunk in a tavern and fallen down some stairs to his death; a woman of unknown provenance, who had been viciously assaulted and left to perish in an alley; and an older man, wearing fine clothes, who had been pulled from the river, bloated and stinking.

The priest was the first claimed—the very afternoon the Mannuary youth was set out—another of the faith coming to the mortuary when the man failed to show up for regular service. The husband of the assaulted woman, a millner, came just as the mortuary assistant was closing the room for the day, along with his two daughters. The legless old man was removed the next morning, as the harlot was brought in by the magistracy, having sat on display for the required three days. Though he was known on the street where he had begged, he had no kin to claim him. The Chief Magistrate contacted a nearby temple and had them arrange a suitable burial.

None of the three remaining bodies were claimed in the next two days, though many people arrived at the mortuary to view them. It was something of a sport among people of a certain class, to come and look upon the unfortunate dead who had perished with no one aware of their passing. Some would concoct outrageous tales about the demise, while others simply thrilled at the idea of being so near the grotesqueness and violence of life on the streets of Dugar.

Two of these arrived late on the third day the Mannurary youth was on display, a young couple in their finery on an afternoon stroll by the look of them. They came first to the older man, wearing clothes not unlike theirs, studying him with an unusual avidity.

"So this is how it has ended," the man said in a low undertone, something like anger or bitterness in his voice.

"He smells as though he has been rotting for weeks," the woman said, wrinkling her nose.

The man called over the assistant on duty and inquired as to where the man had been discovered. "They pulled him out of the river just downstream from Gasnon. He got tangled up in the docks somehow or he'd still be going now."

The assistant wandered away, leaving the couple alone with the body. The woman watched him go, breathing out to her companion. "Who got to him, do you think?"

The man shrugged, his eyes still on the corpse. "Who's to say? Gavisher, I suppose."

"We have to get out Dagar while we still can."

"Not without what is owed us. I didn't sweat blood just to abandon that treasure."

"He'll be after us, darling."

"No doubt," the man said, with a curt nod. "No doubt, to be sure." He stepped away from the body and moved over to study the harlot, pulling the woman along behind him. "Best not to linger, in case Gavisher has people watching the mortuary."

The woman gave half a nod, unable to quite pull her gaze from the older man. "What if he still has the papers on him?"

"What do you suppose her tale is?" the man said, in a voice pitched so that the others in the room might hear it, as he looked upon the harlot. Under his breath, he said, "It doesn't matter. We have no means of getting it. There are too many eyes here. Besides, if Gavisher has any sense, he already has them."

"Perhaps," the woman said, though she sounds doubtful. She looked upon the face of the harlot, doubt and other unnameable thoughts haunting her face. "If that's the case, we should already be gone. Without the papers what good is the treasure?"

"We'll make it work. There's more than one paperman in the world."

She did not reply, going from the harlot to the final body. The Mannuary youth. The man lingered by the harlot, lost in thought, turning only when he heard her gasp of shock. He hurried to her side, taking her by the arm.

"What is it?" he said, though he could see immediately what had drawn such a reaction from her.

"Nothing." She hesitated. "It's just he's so young and looks like my brother."

The man gave a conciliatory murmur and squeezed her shoulder, before leaving her to look closely over the youth's body. His eyes were rapt in concentration and he did not see the assistant approach.

"Is everything all right here?"

"Oh yes, I'm sorry," the woman sniffed. "It's just he looks like my brother you see. How did he come to perish?"

"Passed in the storm the other night, they say," the assistant said. He remained near the body and the man took the woman by the arm and led her away, stopping so that they stood back a bit from the bodies.

"There are no marks, but it is Gavisher's work, no doubt. He must have magicked him on the way to rendezvous."

"What will we do now?"

"We have no choice," the man said, his eyes distant. "We have to try regardless."

Doubt shadowed the woman's face, replaced a moment later by a firm resolution, her eyes hard. By the time the man turned from the body it had vanished and they left, arm in arm.

MAIL ORDER

Daniel threw the mail on table by the door as he came in. "I'm home babe," he called out as he took off his shoes.

"Hey good looking," Alice said, coming over to kiss him. She picked up the mail. "Anything good?"

"Junk. How was your day?"

Alice did not answer. She was engrossed in a postcard-size, glossy mailout advertising a beauty seminar. Daniel had glanced at it while rifling through the mail downstairs, but hadn't noticed anything that would warrant that kind of scrutiny. He went to the kitchen and got a beer from the fridge, cracking it open.

"So how was it babe?" he said, taking a long pull.

"How was what?" Alice said, in a distracted voice, still reading over the mailout.

"Your day."

"Oh, it was fine," Alice said, setting down the mail and looking up at him to smile. "How was yours?"

Daniel shrugged and took another drink of beer. "Same old. What are you thinking for supper?"

After dinner, when Daniel went to put the mail in the recycling, he noticed the mailout was missing.

"You thinking of attending that seminar?" he said, when he came back into the apartment.

"What seminar?"

"The one from the mail. The one you were looking at."

"Oh no," Alice said, laughing. "I thought I recognized the name of the company. I think maybe a friend of mine works there. I was going to look it up."

Daniel grunted in response and went to turn on the television. Alice watched him for a moment, biting her lip. When Daniel glanced up from the television she smiled and he smiled in turn.

Alice looked up at the building number to confirm she was in the right place. 1415, the reverse of the number on the mailout. And she was on 17th Street, not 71st Avenue. She had briefly been worried that Daniel would realize the address on the card was fake, there being no 71st Avenue in Calgary. He had definitely noticed her interest in it and had been curious about it. Fortunately he hadn't pressed her on the matter.

The building was a small office tower filled with innocuous seeming businesses. Law and accounting firms. Counseling agencies. Financial advisers. And the LeBreton Beauty Seminar offices.

They were at the end of a long corridor, lined with a dark green carpet, and filled with closed doors, requiring keycard entry. There was nothing to distinguish any of them, except for the nameplates beside the doors. The carpet was soft and expensive and it hushed her footsteps, making her feel like she was in a library.

She knocked at the door and was received by an impossibly beautiful woman of glacial expressions, who looked Alice over as though she could not possibly belong in a place like this. Alice fished out the card she had received and handed it over.

"One moment please," the woman said and retreated behind her desk. She murmured something into a phone, eyeing her computer screen. Glancing up, she gestured to Alice. "They'll see you now."

Alice proceeded past the front desk and some empty cubicles to a conference room at the back. It had been converted into an office with three work stations. There were two women there, busy at their computers. One looked up as Alice entered.

"You're activated now," she said, without any preamble.

Alice nodded, gulping at the air. The woman got up from her chair and passed her a piece of paper covered with typing. It had come from an ancient printer, a dot matrix, or something of that sort. She hadn't even known those things existed anymore, or that you could get ink for them.

"You have to read it here," the woman said, gesturing to the empty chair. "Once you're done, return it to me."

Alice sat down and read the document over quickly and then a second time more slowly, to take in all the details. When she was done she sighed and read it a third time, to make sure she had not missed anything. She handed it back to the woman who immediately slipped the paper into a shredder and handed her a small envelope.

"Don't open it till later," she said.

Alice left without saying anything. When she passed the front desk the receptionist was murmuring into the phone again. She watched Alice pass by, with the same guarded look and vacant eyes.

Alice did not return home that evening. She drove to the airport and put her car in long term parking. From there she took a taxi to a nearby hotel, checking in for the night. She paid in cash, having already retrieved her alternate identification and travel necessities before going to the meeting that morning. She had hoped that she would be traveling somewhere far away—there was a chance then that she could come back and resume her old life. But there was no possibility of that now.

First, she opened the envelope and studied the business card within, flipping it from side to side as though it might reveal some deeper secrets. Next, she cut up her identification and thoroughly destroyed her phone and anything in her possession that might tie her to her life as Alice. As she did so, she thought of Daniel and about the life she was abandoning. She had always known this day would come. And now it was here. It would be worth it, she told herself. She was a part of a greater whole.

The next day she checked out of her hotel and caught an airport shuttle back to the airport. From there she took transit back to downtown, after picking up a burner phone, not far from where she lived. Had lived, she had to remind herself.

She made her way to a coffee shop and ordered a flat white and sat down to wait, taking care to note everyone who entered as she pretended to peruse her phone. An older man with close-cropped grey hair, a simmering handsomeness and a barely contained physicality entered, glancing about the room. She felt her heart sink a little, though she couldn't have said why. Her initial impression proved correct as he came over to sit across from her.

"I thought I recognized you," he said. "Ana, right?"

She smiled in turn. "Yes. Darryl? From Treehorn?"

"Yeah. How's the conference services world?" Darryl said, sitting across from her.

"Busy, always busy. Have to keep those clients happy," she said, waving her hand at her cell phone.

"Doing any work with anyone I know?" he said. He had contrived to sit at an angle so that he too could see everyone coming and going from the cafe. No one was paying any attention to them. Why would they? Even Alice was bored by this conversation, whose hidden imports she understood.

"Do you know Technique Finances? Gerald McCarthur? LeBreton connected me with him. He's doing a lot of stuff in your line of work. He's in town this week for a payroll systems conference. Might be worth trying to connect with him."

"You have his phone number?"

"I have his card I think," Alice said, reaching into her purse and pulling out the card from the envelope. She passed it across to him, their fingers touching briefly.

"Thanks, I'll give him a call today," Darryl said. He was already standing as he spoke, his eyes staring past her, already on to the next thing.

Alice watched him as he went to order a coffee and left, without glancing in her direction again. He got into a dark sports car and drove away. Alice stared out the window long after he had gone. She needed to be going herself, she knew, but for some reason she could not find the energy. If she started walking now, she could be home in twenty minutes. Walk back into her life, as though she had never left it.

That wasn't possible though. She took a sip of her coffee and found that it was cold. She left it on the table and walked out of the cafe, starting down the street.

CONQUISTADORS

"The world's a simple place, once you understand it. People will talk of Our Lord—and they're right to. Make no mistake, we are His chosen. They'll talk of humility and kindness and justness. All the things they think we should be. But in the end, what matters is who can take what. Remember that. If you can take something—take it. Because rest assured, you'll be a fool to think someone else won't."

The man speaking these words wore a finely tailored doublet, though a close inspection would reveal it was worn and faded, as were the rest of his clothes. His name was Don Luis Farajo, and he led his companion—a ladino youth named Juan—along a winding trail that passed through villages with names he did not know.

"Now that's something your kind just don't understand. Oh, you listen to all the priests have to tell you, I've no doubt. How else did you learn our tongue, after all? But you take it all on faith. You trust. Damned fools, the lot of you. Look at Atahualpa with Pizarro. He had no intention of keeping his word. None. Yet the whole empire was lost because an emperor did not understand the fundamental rule of the world. Takers always take. And always will. Mark my words."

Juan did not answer Don Luis, his eyes on the trail ahead. It was early morning, the sun still climbing above the mountains which towered around them. They had started off before dawn from the inn they had spent the night in, passing men and women carrying goods for the day's market down the steep paths they were climbing. It was exhausting work and Juan chewed coca leaves to ward off his appetite, though Don Luis scoffed at his habit, calling it uncivilized.

Don Luis had opinions on all matters, which he was never shy to share with anyone who happened to be at hand. Especially Juan, who he seemed to view as a child who he had a solemn duty to properly educate in the ways of the world. This despite the fact Juan could speak Spanish as well as any Peninsular, having been taught by the Dominican friars he served in Pisac. Of the two of them it was Juan who had the rudiments of his letters, though the ladino never dared mention that to Don Luis.

"See, now pay mind to these people," Don Luis said, gesturing at the family that was making its way down the hill, their backs heavy with baskets filled with alpaca wool clothes. "They have not done a thing different than their fathers or their father's fathers in all their lives. Wake up and walk down to the valley. Spend the day at market and then go back up. Now, you at least have started your education. Those friars taught you a thing or two.

"But so many men—even Spaniards, by God—can't be bothered to do more than what their fathers did. And what do you think they accomplished? Nothing. No, I will not be like them. Not me. I've seen to that. Come across to this New World and these godforsaken villages. But we won't be idling here long, will we Juan?"

Juan agreed with a murmur. The sun was up above the mountains now, burning bright and warm, and both men were soon covered in a sheen of sweat. They continued up further, past the last of the villages, until they could see the ruins standing above it all. It was a grand fortress, still standing strong, as though it might be able to repel the Spaniards simply by its existence, each stone intricately placed against the next, creating a vast whole.

There were row upon row of terraces extending below the stones of the fortress and the two men made their way up them until they arrived at the foot of the fortress. Once there, Don Luis led the way to the river that curved around the far side of the ruins. An old bridge extended across it, leading to a hillside that had once had a few houses built into it. There were also a number of, what appeared to be, caves whose entrances had been blocked over with stone. It was to these that the two men went.

"See, now this is the kind of thing people don't think about. It takes a certain mind to see the opportunity here. Your people, they just see a sacred place, to be respected. Nonsense. The dead are dead. They'll continue to lie there regardless of what you, God or anyone else does. Now, my people, they're off looking for the next empire—El Dorado, or whatever such thing they think exists over the next hill. Nonsense too. We don't need an El Dorado to make our fortunes. We just need the right grave, the right bit of treasure. And here, I think, we'll have it."

Don Luis stopped in front of one of the stone walls and gestured for Juan to hand him one of the picks he carried. Together they started to work on breaking the stones, the sound of metal on rock echoing from the mountain down into the valley below. When they had cleared enough of the wall away, Don Luis lit a candle he had stuffed in one of his pockets and slipped into the hole, casting the light around to see what was there.

Juan followed after him, making a sign of the cross. A body, mummified and dressed in ancient clothes lay on a stone at the center of the cavern. Don Luis ignored it, rooting through the rest of grave, which was filled with various artifacts, his eyes alert only for the glimmer of gold. They found none in the first grave, or in the second, but the third and fourth revealed a few small trinkets which the Spaniard pocketed.

"You see Juan. It's just as I said. There is a fortune here for the taking. Those other fools running around the jungle never bother to get their hands a little dirty here. And your people don't want to disturb the dead. That's foolish. The dead are dead. They will lie there regardless."

Juan did not think that was the case, but he offered no comment. They busied themselves with opening the fifth grave, which proved to be the largest. It contained a stunning number of tiny figurines crafted from gold and silver. Some were shaped as men and women, others as jaguars, alpacas or other beasts. There were so many the sack Juan carried was almost too heavy to carry.

Don Luis danced about with glee, unable to contain himself. "My fortune is made boy. It is made. Think of what I can do with the coin from this. There might even be enough here to let me buy some land in Spain. You see, it's just as I said. The reward will always go to those who take."

Juan paid no mind to Don Luis. He was studying the figurines under the candlelight. As he did so he had a vision of himself picking up one of the stones they had knocked loose and striking Don Luis in the head, leaving him here so that he might take the gold for himself. The Spaniard would never expect it. Juan could pile up the rocks, restoring the wall, so that Don Luis would be trapped. By the time he managed to get himself free, if he ever did, Juan would have disappeared.

Something stayed his hand, though it was a tempting vision. Juan could not say what it was. Perhaps it was the teaching of the Dominicans, who would surely disapprove of such an act, just as they would consider both Juan and Don Luis the pair of scoundrels they were. Or perhaps it was just that he did not believe what Don Luis said about the ways of the world. There were other ways, other paths, and he would find his own.

"Come Juan," Don Luis said, stepping out of the tomb back into the light. "We'll have to hurry if we're to be back to civilization by nightfall. We don't want to be on the open road with this gold. Takers will take, as I say."

Juan slipped a few of the figurines from the sack into his own pockets and followed Don Luis down the mountain.

MENU DEL DÍA

Gerald grimaced against the glare of the sun as he stared down the teeming street. The faces shifted rapidly across his frame of vision, the calls of the hawkers drowning out any chatter on the street that the clatter of the vehicles trundling by did not. He bit his lip as his stomach was lanced by a sharp pain that shuddered down his bowels and threatened to spill out at his feet.

"Everything okay?" Ariel said.

"Yeah," he said, exhaling slowly and relaxing his tense muscles, hoping nothing dislodged itself in the process.

She laughed. "That bad, huh?"

"Fucking menu del día. Never should've eaten that."

"I warned you," Ariel said.

"Oh god," Gerald said, clutching at his stomach. "Now is definitely not the time."

"You still up for the museum?"

"Not like we've got another day. Bound to be a bathroom in there anyway."

Ariel led the way along the uneven cobblestone street, past the Incan wall with its massive many-sided stones, to what had once been the Archbishop's palace. Now it was a museum filled with works of cusqueño art from the colonial period, though there were still Church offices on site. The archbishop continued to attend there on occasion. They had bought a ticket for the museum the day before at the cathedral on the main square and now they had the ticket punched and were offered an audio tour, which Ariel accepted, procuring headphones for both of them.

They went from room to room of the palace, which had been home to an Incan priest prior to the Church taking it over, following the conquest, listening to their audio guide drone on about the minutia of the art work on the walls. It all looked much the same to Gerald, paeans to God, Mary and Jesus, intended to educate those new to the faith by placing these foreign symbols in familiar contexts. Thus, there was a guinea pig, corn and potatoes being served with every image of the Last Supper. One example of this would have been enough to make the point, but the paintings seemed to proliferate throughout each room.

Gerald had to allow that the paintings were incredible, though he always found the baroque effects left him cold. He was especially unmoved on this day because of the rather tenuous state of his stomach. It was a matter of when, not if, he would need a bathroom, and he had yet to see a sign directing him to one.

There was a courtyard at the building's center, with a garden filled with flowers and trees, as well as a random assortment of colonial artifacts left to brave the elements. Leaving Ariel to listen to the audio guide, he passed around the entire courtyard looking for a sign for the washrooms, but did not see one.

"For God sakes," he muttered to himself. There had to be one.

A security guard stood at one corner of the courtyard, looking studiously indifferent. Gerald approached him. "Hay un baño acquí?"

The guard did not bother with a reply, shaking his head no. Gerald turned away, his stomach choosing that moment to roil in agony again. His innards felt like a ship lost in a storm, with no sense of where they might end up or whether or not they would be cast asunder. He had to stop and wait, to be certain it had passed, before he could safely go on.

Wandering back into the rooms, he found Ariel engrossed in a painting depicting a scene of a procession through the streets, mirroring the life of some saint or another. A representation of a devil or demon could be seen in one corner, though his face had been blurred beyond recognition.

"They removed the face because it was some important noble. His enemy had it done," Ariel whispered to him, though they were alone in the room.

"Well, we know all about that," Gerald said. "No baño,"

"We do indeed. No baño?"

"Nope."

"Are you going to be able to make it?" A hint of concern now, along with a bit of anger.

"Of course," Gerald said, wincing as his stomach told him otherwise. *I'll just have to improvise,* he thought, but did not say.

They continued on, Gerald doing his best not to think about his churning stomach. Each time it lurched he would close his eyes and clench himself, hoping to somehow hold back the flow that threatened to burst out. More than once he was certain he had failed, only to realize, with a sort of giddiness that all was well. For the moment.

As he listened to the audio guide droning on about archbishop's offices, he made a decision. He couldn't wait until they returned to the hotel. There had to be bathrooms in the archbishop's offices. They took shits the same as everyone else. Hopefully.

He went back to the courtyard, glancing to make sure the security guard was absent, and ducked through a door he had noted earlier with a sign that said "Oficinas." He found himself in a corridor lined with offices on either side. Not a bathroom in sight.

"Goddammit," he whispered through clenched teeth. Sweat formed on his forehead.

He reached the end of the hallway and followed it right. More offices. Maybe they didn't shit like everyone else, Gerald thought to himself. It was no longer funny. Every step felt like it could lead to disaster.

It was only at the end of hallway, which turned another corner into a secluded alcove, that he discovered the washroom. He burst in, not even bothering to check if it was the men's or the women's, and threw himself into a stall. His fingers seemed incapable of undoing his belt or unzipping his fly, even as his body surrendered to the inevitable. He didn't even have time to sit on the toilet before it burst out. Liquid agony. Everywhere.

When it was finished his relief was ecstatic. Every muscle in his body seemed to unclench. He wanted to weep. Even as he luxuriated in this bliss, his stomach grumbled, promising more struggles to come.

He would deal with those when they came. For now, he had work to do. He slipped out of the washroom and went back down the hallway, until he came to the door he had noted his first time by. It was locked and, after a quick glance down the corridor to confirm he was alone, he set about opening it with his credit card. The telltale click came a moment later and he slipped within.

The room was some official's office, though it was not immediately obvious who. Gerald did not know and did not care. He went to the filing cabinet that stood in the corner and knelt at the bottom drawer. It was locked as well, but a quick search of desk drawers produced a key. The drawer was crammed with files and Gerald picked through them carefully, until he saw the name he was looking for.

He pulled the file out and slipped it under his shirt, returning back the way he had come. When he emerged into the courtyard there were a few tourists taking pictures who looked at him strangely. Gerald ignored them and wandered through the rooms until he found Ariel.

"Everything good?" Her tone was light, her nervousness only betrayed by the slightest tremor.

"Yes, but we should get moving."

She nodded and smiled. "Not going to make it much longer?"

"No, I've lasted about as long as I can."

They passed through the final rooms to the front desk, where the security guard idled, chatting with the girl at the ticket desk. Ariel returned the audio guide, while Gerald waited outside. When she was done, they started up the street to the city's main square, disappearing into the crowd.

THE DAME

"There's a woman here to see you. Real looker." Daisy said, sticking her head in through Murphy's door.

Murphy nodded to send her in. He got a good look at her as she came in through the door. Eyes downcast to look demur, but there was a light to them that said otherwise. Her lips were the kind that always seemed to be smiling, or on the verge of it. A beautiful girl, no doubt about it.

"What can I do for you Miss...?"

"Adeline Sandos. Thank you for seeing me, Mr. Murphy. I have a problem. I'm not quite sure how to explain it."

"Just start at the beginning," Murphy said, with a generous smile, his eyes intent upon her.

Adeline hesitated, looking away and then back at Murphy. "Well, it's my husband, you see." Murphy nodded, as though he had expected her to say that. "He's gotten mixed up with some bad people I think. And I'm worried..."

Here she hesitated again. Murphy leaned forward slightly. "What worries you, Miss Sandos?"

"Well, I'm worried there may be another woman."

Murphy nodded, as though he had expected that too. He made her tell him everything, even those things she seemed reluctant to talk about, asking questions about particular details. When he was done he sent her on her way with some reassurance, telling her to put a retainer down with Daisy. He watched her leave the room, his eyes lingering on her as she left, his lips pursed in thought.

Adeline left the detective agency and took a cab across town to the Hotel Bellmire, an old and majestic place downtown that seemed a little faded, as though it were a picture on a postcard that had sat in the sun too long. She did not stop at the front desk, heading straight up to the fifth floor where she let herself into one of the rooms. The Brides were waiting for her there.

They were a set of twins, handsome and youthful, though less youthful upon closer inspection, with glittering eyes and smiles with edges.

"How did it go?" one said.

"Just like you said," Adeline said. "I told him everything, just like you told me to to tell it."

"And he didn't suspect you of anything?"

Adeline shook her head. "It didn't matter what I said. A whiff of innocence and desperation was all he needed. He was in all the way."

"Good girl. Fix her a drink," the one brother said.

The first brother glared at him, as if to tell him to do it himself, but he got up and poured Adeline a whiskey. She drank it off in one gulp.

"There's the matter of my payment," she said, fixing them both with a steady eye.

"All in due time, all in due time."

Adeline shook her head. "How about now instead?"

The first Bride brother gave her a thin smile. "Very well." He fished an envelope from within the breastpocket of his suit and handed it to her.

Ignoring the two men, Adeline counted out the bills. She glanced up at them. "This is half what I'm owed."

"Yes, you see our little scheme is only workable if you make yourself scarce. You will do so tonight and, at the conclusion of the affair, you will receive the remainder of what was agreed."

"This wasn't the agreement," Adeline said, shaking her head. "I get it all now, or I leave here and go straight to the police and sing my song."

"That would be unwise," the first brother said, with a disapproving shake of his head. The second brother pulled a pistol out from the waistband of his suit. "Most unwise."

Adeline looked at the gun and shook her head. "You think you can scare me? You don't need a body on your hands. You need me gone."

"That can be arranged."

"Not the way you want it, or we wouldn't be having this conversation. No, you're not going to kill me. Too messy. Too easy to tie to you. I made sure to talk to the front desk and let them know whose room I was headed to. So, I'll just take the rest of what we agreed and be on my way to disappearing. Otherwise, you can expect visits from Murphy and the police."

The second brother cocked the pistol and raised it up so that it was pointed directly at Adeline's head. She stared at him without blinking, her face expressionless.

The first brother made a disgusted sound and waved at the other. "Put that away. We can't be taking chances at this juncture of the affair. Very well, Miss Sandos." He pulled out a thick roll of bills from his suit pocket and counted off ten. "This should square us, I think."

Adeline tucked them into the envelope with the rest. "Pleasure doing business, gents," she said with a curt nod. "You won't be seeing me."

She turned, not bothering to wait for a reply, and headed for the door.

Murphy was waiting for her when she returned home.

"See, I knew it didn't check out," Murphy said to her, an amused, but superior expression on his face. The cat that had the mouse in its paws and was going to play awhile. "It smelled a little funny. All of it. And then I get to looking into you and it seems there is an Adeline Sandos, but you ain't her. And that's when I knew the Bride boys were up to something."

Adeline's face betrayed no emotion. "Am I supposed to congratulate you now, or something?"

"What are they about? What's their game?"

"Shouldn't you be over there asking them that?"

"In due time," Murphy said. "In due time. First, there's some things I need you to clear up."

Adeline sighed. "They sent me. I'm supposed to disappear and cause you some problems. That's my end of it. Anything else you want to know?"

Murphy seemed taken aback. He swallowed, his triumph not

seeming so complete now. "Why are you telling me this?"

"It's not my problem their little scheme is blowing up in their face. I got my money. Now run along and confront them. They're probably hoping you will anyway. That's what you all want isn't it?"

Murphy frowned, but he stood and put his hat on his head. "Just tell me your end of it," he said, shaking his head.

Adeline laughed. "I already told you. I got paid. Now, you don't want to keep those boys waiting. I'm sure there'll be a lot of yelling and threats and such."

Murphy looked as though he wanted to disagree with her, but instead he walked out the door, leaving her alone. Adeline pulled out the wad of bills from the envelope and tucked them underneath the coffee cup at the back of one of the cupboards. Then she pulled out a bottle of whiskey and poured herself a shot.

THE BARE SCENT

Richard shot Matthews once, in the neck, and stood and watched as he crumpled to the floor, his breath coming in gurgles as the blood leaked out of him at a frightening pace. The sound of the shot had startled him. It had been both louder and quieter than he had expected. He stayed watching as Matthews bled out, his eyes blinking rapidly while he tried to speak, thinking only that he had been aiming for the head, not the neck.

Finally he remembered himself and, dropping the gun beside the dying man, he turned on his heels and walked out of the room, down the hallway, to the stairs. He moved at a steady pace, as though he had a purpose and was on his way somewhere, but he encountered no one. It was two flights to the main floor where he exited the stairwell into the hotel lobby and calmly walked out past the bellhops, desk attendants and guests, drawing not a single glance, through the revolving door and out into the glare of the sun.

There were two cabs parked out front and he got into the first one, giving the man an address—the first one that came into his head, a restaurant he had looked up the night before. The cab pulled out into the flow of traffic and Richard sucked in a deep breath, what felt like his first in a long while. He looked down at his hands and saw that they were shaking, and then realized that no, that was an illusion. It was his vision itself that was unsteady. The whole world was vibrating.

"You visiting town?" the cab driver said, in a way that suggested it was not the first time he had asked Richard the question.

Richard met the driver's eyes in the rearview mirror. *Don't say anything memorable. Say nothing.* "Yeah. Just for a couple of days."

"Business? Pleasure?" He had an accent Richard could not quite place.

"A little of both actually. I hope."

"Ahh, yes," the driver said with a vigorous nod. "I know, I know. Meetings all day and then party all night, right?"

"Something like that," Richard said, growing uncomfortable.

He looked away from the mirror, out the window and then down at his shoes. To his horror he could see a drop of blood on the toe of one shoe, glaringly red against its blackness. He glanced up at the driver, but his eyes were on the road, apparently oblivious to Richard's concern.

"You know," the driver said, in an overly casual voice. "I know a guy got some girls and such. Whatever you want. Whatever you need for a party."

Richard could not stop looking at his shoe. He desperately wanted to lean down and clean it off, but he didn't know what to do with the blood once it was on his fingers.

"Sure," he found himself saying. "Where are these girls at?"

He felt his orgasm building with each thrust and resultant moan from the girl beneath him. She was Puerto Rican, according to her, lovely and thin and lithe, and she wriggled her body beneath him in a way that seemed exceptional to him, though he could not have said why exactly. Nothing seemed exact at the moment. There had been a number of shots of cheap whiskey and a bump of cocaine before he had started in on this girl.

Monique. Not her real name. Nothing was real, at least not that he could be sure. The blood on his shoe, for instance, had not been there when he at last worked up the courage to wipe it off on the cab ride over here. The driver had been even more gregarious by then, already counting his cut of Richard's afternoon in his head. There had been a number of watchful eyes in the apartment, all waiting for some sign that he was not who he appeared to be. That much, at least, was true.

It did not matter. Matthews was gone. A debt repaid. He felt a bit of the blood go from his cock at that thought and tried to return his focus to Monique. She smiled at him, urging him on, but her eyes were empty. Dead. It was that thought that finally sent his orgasm spilling out and he collapsed on top of her, their sweat mingling.

"I'm missing my flight," he said, for what seemed to be the hundredth time. It was true. Nothing else was. All other existence was fragments of pieces of things that might have once happened. No one could say for sure.

"You think I give a fuck," the voice said. "Do you know how much that cost? Why would I care about you missing a goddamn flight? Now you are gonna fucking pay me."

Richard blinked at the voice, but it refused to coalesce into a face. He was confused by what the voice had said. He had paid for the whore, that much he was certain of. And the cocaine. And the whiskey. Then what was this about? Matthews.

"How did you find me?" This point seemed very central to the entire matter. Richard needed it clarified.

The voice sighed. It sounded tired. "You spent two nights pussy deep instead of getting the fuck out of town. How do you think we found you?"

Richard nodded. It made sense.

"Why the fuck did you kill Matthews, you dumbshit?"

Matthews, yes. Why had he shot Matthews? It seemed very unimportant now, a distant concern. There was that flight he had to catch. That was paramount, though he could not remember where he was flying to.

"Listen to me fuckwit," the voice said. It was a different voice actually. There were in fact two voices, he realized. "Why did you kill Matthews? Who hired you? Do you understand how important he is to certain people? You are royally fucked unless you talk to us."

Richard did talk, though it all came out in a babble. Not even he understood it. He could feel his lips and tongue moving, but it was a distant sensation, separate from his thoughts. Nothing was real. Not this, not the whore, not Matthews. None of it. He was just drifting on a river further into the darkness. A ship awaited him there, to carry him across the sea.

"Jesus Christ. What did you do?"

"Nothing for fuck sakes. I didn't touch him."

Richard tried to blink, but the light was too dim. The sea was very cold.

"Check his pulse."

"He doesn't have one. Jesus, he's cold."

"We need him alive. We need to know who hired him."

Richard smiled. There was a scent, the bare scent of Monique's flesh as he had lain atop her. He could smell it now. She must have gone out for some more whiskey. He closed his eyes to wait for her to join him.

THE SERVANT

A flash of lightning on the horizon as dusk settles upon those vast peaks that spread in all directions. It forms a haunting visage of a land torn apart, uprooted and broken, seized by unspeakable forces in days long ago. Ves slides down a snow-streaked road that winds into the town below, his journey interrupted from time to time by the surge of lights from a vehicle making an ascent. The town is quiet, the streets nearly empty, but for a few revelers gathered at the foot of a stairway leading up to a tavern. There are shouts from within and the promise of warmth, drink and women, but he passes on. His day is not yet done.

The town is built upon a mountain with streets that slant here and there, coming together at odd angles, or sometimes ending abruptly. It is one of these that Ves finds himself on, the road coming to an end at a cliff, the gulf below stretching on into a darkness that seems to know no bounds. At the precipice of this awful vastness sits a mansion, spreading across the cliff so broadly that it gives the impression it might teeter over the brink at any moment to what lies below.

When he announces himself at the door servants scurry to rouse the Master. Ves is taken through the building and brought out onto a veranda overlooking the precipice. The air is cool and he can see his breath forming under the lights. He does not have to wait long until the Master emerges from one of the doors to join him. He is unremarkable to look upon, small and thin, with fine features that somehow leave him undefined. Ves can rarely call up

178

a picture of his face in his mind.

"So you found her, did you?" the Master says.

Ves nods. "She has a message for you."

The Master gestures for him to continue and Ves reaches into his pocket and removes the ring he has kept there these last long months and holds it out for the Master. He takes it and holds it up between his fingers to study it, the ring flashing under the glare of the veranda lights.

"Unfortunate," the Master says. "How many is that now?"

"Fifteen," Ves says.

The Master sighs. He looks very old for a moment, carefully hidden years emerging from within his flesh. "I fear our hour grows later and later."

Ves does not reply, knowing the Master refers only to himself. He will outlive this man, he will last as long as these mountains. As if thinking the same thing, the Master turns to Ves. "Who will you serve when I am gone?

Ves does not answer. The Master does not require an answer, and he could not give him one even if he did.

"You are very much a present tense sort of creature, Ves," the Master says with a smile, though his voice holds no amusement. Once again Ves does not speak. "What did she say to you?"

"She said your time has passed, that the universe will go on without you running it. Your power has vanished and it is time someone else took your place."

The Master shakes his head, looking out into the implacable darkness beyond the cliff. "Of course she did. And I imagine she thinks she is the one to be in charge now. Did she make an offer to you?"

Ves nods. The Master flinches at that motion, though he quickly recovers. "And what did you say to her?"

In response Ves reaches out to seize the Master, ignoring his cry of anger and fear, and sends him off the veranda over the precipice, hurtling into the abyss below. His screams seem endless, though eventually they dim and quiet, the serenity of the mountain evening is restored. Ves stares into the unfathomable darkness below, contemplating it for a time. When he is done he nods at it, as though acknowledging someone, and turns back toward the mansion.

There are several of the Masters other servants standing at the veranda door watching him with trepidation, drawn by the Master's scream. When they see him turn around they flee back into the house, glancing back as if expecting Ves to follow. He does not, going to sit on one of the veranda chairs, staring off at the sky as though lost in thought. After half an hour or more a new star appears above, growing larger and brighter by the moment and Ves stands and heads into the mansion.

Within the other servants are frantically packing what they can and streaming from the house out into the mountain town. Though it is many hours before dawn, most start down the tortuous road to the valley below. Some are weeping, all look frightened and grim, already appearing to be destitute in spite of the finery of their clothes. Ves pays them little mind, standing aside to let them go.

When the last is gone, Ves closes the door and stands outside at the entrance, erect and alert, his eyes still on the growing star. The light grows brighter and brighter until it blinks out, disappearing into the planet's darkside. Some time later he hears the roar of a landing vessel echoing through the mountains. Its lights are visible a moment later and he watches as it sets down on the landing pad just above the town.

Soon there are a number of people, marching in a line, down the road and the streets he had recently walked, visible but unrecognizable from the streetlights. Ves knows who they are and he sets his vest, smoothing out his shirt and pants, and goes out to greet his new Master.

DIME NOVEL DENOUEMENT

This moment does not seem to be a moment. It seems endless, interminable. An internment camp. The holding pen before the gulag. Devoid creatures wander through the night along empty streets, straying from the light. I am one of them now.

Rain begins to fall, softly at first, and then in staccato bursts. I scuttle across openings, clinging to the security of the damp mildewed walls. There are eyes everywhere, but none look for me. I am worth nothing to anyone. No price will be paid. Yet, I refuse to expose myself. I am no martyr, whatever else I may be.

You speak and I shiver and clutch my hands in my pocket. This parched feeling that holds and won't let go. I fight for words; silence is like a wound, like a lie I always tell. You do not care whether I speak or stay quiet, all you care is what I do.

The thousand betrayals of a life leave the birth of the malformed. I've clawed at my own skin, it does not fit right. Nature seems dead and wicked dreams abuse.

I'm looking for a taste of ecstasy, I've had delight and it lost its potency. With you at my side on this long, damp and dark road.

I long to taste the sunrise in your mouth, as my tongue slides past your teeth and the morning dew is fresh on my lips. I want to smell your sweat on me, the heat of my flesh on the heat of yours, shivering, shimmering to a glow.

Oh, to look upon you now, through the blur of the rain. If I could take you in this doorway I would.

The light is dim and furtive. I am gaping and madcap, nothing more than a distorted reflection in a pool of water, spun out of spells. Only a shadow of the feeling remains, as though a cloud were passing over the sun.

I am spun out of spells. The missionary cast them all out, leaving the rains to come alone. I no longer hear the words, they are empty to me. There were things I once said, worlds I made dance, that are gone to me now. Once my voice could make mountains tremble. Or so I said. I am left with this and the cheapness of it appalls me.

I remember waking up and chewing off my hand, stumbling out into the dregs of the morning, smoke rising up from the wretched hovels, sprawled in misery across the valley floor. Those foul and terrible places I bore witness to. The yelps and cries of the twisted masses, torn from bleeding and bruised lips.

The ripped limbs, the misshapen holes, that peered into nothingness, that disappeared utterly into the shuddering entrails of convulsing minds.

What is left there now? What is left anywhere? Only the trail I now follow, this wandering pair, waiting for it to become one.

Let me tell you about being here, looking out at the gleam of streetlights from behind your curtains.

I am as undeniable as a summer breeze. You are as inevitable as a final sigh, seeing the sun move across the horizon. I can feel your body. Can you hear the whispers I speak?

It cannot be for eternity. But winter is a long time, and it is enough to be here beside you now, even if just for this moment.

We're all of us a little incomplete, not quite there, shining and corrupt darkness. A gaping obscenity. Out there, they are hacking one another, survival at a whim, the mere percussion of chance. So we say to each other. It is easier that way.

I approach him with this sneer of destruction, of the coming, unsuspected massacre. Hands tied behind his back, shot in the face, lying scattered about on the broken ground. Walked out and down the road, blood washing off me slowly in the rain.

I wanted something else, not a dime novel conclusion. Reservations lost, the far side of the sky all filled up. You smile at me, in that offhand kind of way.

We have been bodies, we have been bodies, we are not shapes anymore.
I hear a fumbling organ in the distance. You look at me as though there are possibilities.

LAST STAND

THE SUPREME EFFECT

Morning light crept along the horizon, expanding further with each passing moment its domain, revealing the outlines of trees. There was a trail leading through the trees into a meadow, well-worn by the shepherds and the cattle and sheep they brought here to graze. They were absent this early, not yet stirring in their beds miles away. The grass was heavy with moisture and even as the light grew, the air turned misty and a bank of fog settled over the landscape, obscuring the trees and making the trail difficult to pick out.

Four figures emerged from the fog and stood across from each other. No one spoke or moved for a time, all of them staring at each other with a mixture of unease and disdain, bravado and fear. As the fog began to dissipate, an unspoken signal passed between them and two of the men stepped together to stand between the remaining two, bowing formally to each other. The two solitary men backed away from the pair in opposite directions until they were almost lost to each other in the murk.

"Brach wishes to commence?" one of the pair said.

The other nodded, his mouth formed into a thin grimace. They both wore dark robes, similar in cut and design. Their heads were shaved and their faces clean-cut. Their age was indeterminate; they appeared young, but something about their youth was edged with the entropy of years. The only thing to distinguish them was that one had blue eyes and the other brown.

"Hjesch as well," the one with the blue eyes said.

"Then let us commence," the brown-eyed second said. "We agree that the duel shall be without assistance? There will be no implements or engines, no familiars, and we, of course, shall remain observers only."

"Agreed. As Hjesch has chosen the place, Brach can choose the element."

"Water," was The brown-eyed second's immediate response.

The blue-eyed second nodded curtly. "A fine day for it. We further stipulate the battle shall involve no non-magical implements."

"Of course. Are we fighting to first blood? To supreme effect?"

"To the death," the blue-eyed second said and they both shared a faint smile, as though he had uttered a joke.

"If it is all agreed to your satisfaction," The brown-eyed second said, "I suggest we inform the duelists and begin the contest."

The other bowed slightly and they both turned to walk the several paces toward their respective parties to whisper the particulars of their agreement. When both men had agreed, the two seconds walked back to their original positions together between the two combatants. Each raised their left arm high in the air, looking to the duelists to ensure they could spot them through the fog. After a pause where they stood, arms poised, during which the mist halted and sun pierced somewhat through the fog, they both dropped their arms, in a scything motion, to their sides and the battle was engaged.

Nothing happened for several moments, both combatants eyeing each other as best they could. The fog grew thicker and the mist heavier, obscuring them both as well as the seconds. The air felt charged with electricity that might be unleashed at any moment in a cataclysmic thunderbolt.

No such charge was released, but a cloud, heavy with moisture, engulfed the meadow, subsuming the fog and the mist. It moved as though animated, slithering around Brach, slowly tightening its grasp upon him. Like a snake it began to constrict him, crushing his chest and neck so that he could not breath. The air left his lungs in an strange gasp as the cloud cinched itself tighter and tighter around him.

Oddly, his face betrayed no sign of the distress he must have been experiencing. It was placid and calm, his eyes far-looking upon a horizon he could not possibly see. Only one hand trembled slightly, hinting at the agonies he was undergoing.

Just as it seemed the cloud could grow no thicker, an inescapable morass from which Brach could never escape, an odd cracking sound echoed through the air. As its reverberations died, the cloud surrounding Brach and the two seconds vanished in time for them all to witness the ground opening up at Hjesch's feet, sending him tumbling into a pit deep within the earth.

The two seconds stirred from where they watched the contest and moved toward the pit. They looked down into the impenetrable blackness and were surprised by the bitter cold of the air arising from it, creating small clouds in the air that clung around the pit's edge.

The blue-eyed second grunted. "He cracked the frost. Clever that."

The other did not reply, his eyes intent upon the crevasse that was redolent with the smell of damp earth and decomposition. Neither of them said anything further as they stared into the pit expectantly. The sun had fully risen above the trees, burning off the last of the fog, though the clouds still remained scattered above, casting down a slight drizzle on them. Behind them Brach waited as well, motionless, a faraway gaze in his eyes still.

"Shall we call it?" The blue-eyed second said. There was both disappointment and hope in his voice.

The brown-eyed second shook his head. "Wait," he said.

The minutes stretched on. Birds began to chirp around them, flitting among the grass, which was slowly drying off as even the drizzle ceased. Finally the brown-eyed second turned to the other, his mouth open, ready to speak. Before he could though, Brach gave a mournful cry of defeat and they saw a hand emerge from the pit and then another, as Hjesch pulled himself from the bowels of the earth back into the sunlight.

His robes were dirty and he was unsteady on his feet, but he otherwise appeared fine. The two seconds stared at him, expressionless, no one speaking. They turned to Brach, who at last stirred from where he was and walked over to join them, his own expression unreadable. The four together began to walk along the trail across the meadow and into the trees where they vanished from sight.

MENTHOLS AND PISCO SOUR

She tasted of menthols and pisco sours. Jaime ran his tongue along her lips, savoring the flavor, before biting at her lip. He could feel her freeze a little at the sharpness of the pain, wondering if he was going to go further, and had to resist a smile. She was staring at him, looking up from the circle of his arms, where he pressed her in close.

Looking down at her and meeting her gaze, Jaime was unable to tell what exactly she was thinking. She was not lost in passion, not eager to see that he was either. No, she was watching him, a part of her reserved and standing off, to observe this. What for, he wondered, slightly unsettled. To cover his unease, he bit down on her lip again, harder this time, and was satisfied to see her wince and frown.

She had told him her name, but he did not remember it. They had met in some dive bar near Plaza San Martín in Lima, a dark and grubby place he sometimes went to when he wanted to be with the people, so to speak. It was across the street from a tourist hotel and sometimes he would meet American girls there, who were also deigning to visit the place, looking for a little danger. If only they knew, he thought.

This girl though, he had thought she was a prostitute, off the clock for the night. Or maybe not, maybe the bill would come due in an hour or two. She was light skinned, with mestizo features, and quite beautiful with long black hair, wide eyes and incredible tits. They were what had drawn his attention first. Her teeth were a little crooked and her clothes a little too tight and little too garish. Otherwise he would have expected to find her in one of the Miraflores clubs. Maybe, in a couple of years, if fate shone upon her, he would.

Tired of kissing, Jaime moved to pull down the shoulders of her dress and reveal what he was here for, but she pulled away from him. "I just need to go to the bathroom babe," she said, patting his cock through his jeans. "Don't unload this while I'm gone."

He smiled and released her, or rather, she wiggled from his grasp. He walked over to the bed and sat on it, contemplating taking his clothes off, but decided not to. Let her take them off, that would be more fun. Absentmindedly, he flipped on the television, searching for a sports station while he waited.

They were in a hourly hotel, called El Encuentro, the sort of place where everyone ended up at some point or another. Boyfriends and girlfriends stealing away for that first time. Husband and wives who just wanted some peace from her parents and his children from the first marriage. Affairs, of course, and people like him. Impromptu customers.

As a result, the furnishings were very minimal. There was only a mattress and a sheet and two very flat looking pillows. Beside the bed there was a small table with a phone, and on the other side there was a large tub with jets. The place was immaculately clean. That was why he came here. It was something he looked for.

He flipped through the channels for a second time, unable to find anything to capture his interest. Even the porn channels weren't exciting him. Where the hell was this girl?

As he looked up, determined to go to the bathroom and see for himself what as going on—maybe she was getting high; he didn't like that, not around him—the bathroom door opened and she stepped out. The first thing Jaime noticed was that she had not taken off her dress to reveal those remarkable tits, which irritated him. The second thing was that she had a gun in her hand, which annoyed him even more.

"What the fuck is this?" he said, standing up and glaring at her.

"Stay right there," she said, motioning with the gun.

"Fuck you. I don't know what the fuck you think you're doing, but it's not going to work."

"Isn't it?" she said, smiling coyly. "I have my gun in my hand. Where is yours?"

His hand twitched, betraying him, and her smile widened. "Take it out—slowly—and put it on the floor." He did as she said. "Good. Now kick it over here." Jaime did that as well, grimacing all the while.

She did not bend down to retrieve the weapon, as he had hoped she would, instead kicking it behind her into the bathroom, which she closed. This was all going very badly, but Jaime was still more angry than afraid. It was impossible for him to believe that he would not come out of this alive. People did not just threaten and kill him. That was not what happened.

"Now. Your pants. Gesturing again with her gun.

"My pants?" he said, a small grin touching his lips. "Is this your game girl? Pretty brave, thinking I would go for it."

"I've done my research," she said, her expression unchanged. "Take off your pants and keep your hands where I can see them."

Jaime cursed her, calling her a bitch, a cunt and a whore, but he complied, undoing his belt and dropping his pants to the floor. He worked his way out of them, stepping from side to side, keeping his hands in plain sight. When he was done, she gestured for him to kick them over to her, which he did.

"Shirt," she said.

"Damn girl. You could have just told me to take all my clothes."

"Yes."

Jaime squinted at her while he unbuttoned his shirt. He still was not afraid, still confident he could escape this too. But the woman was intriguing him, he had to admit. No matter what her game ultimately was, he was curious. Somehow he would get answers from her.

He threw the shirt at her feet. "Now what?"

She considered the question a moment. "Underwear too."

"Fuck," Jaime said. "What is with the goddamn process here. Let's just get this over with, why don't we?"

"We are," she said, gesturing again with the gun. "Take off your underwear."

There was something in her tone that unsettled him. She did not sound turned on or excited by this game, which suggested it was not a game. It was something else entirely. He took off his underwear and threw it on top of his shirt.

"There," he said. "Happy? Or do you want the socks too?"

"No," she said. "That will do." She lowered the gun so that it was aimed at his groin and fired.

Jaime screamed and fell to the floor, clutching at his midsection. He could feel blood, warm on his fingers and wanted to look down, but couldn't bear to. The pain was unbelievable. There was a voice cursing the woman, calling her a whore, telling her what he would do to her, the ways he would violate her. It was, Jaime realized, his own voice.

"How are you going to do all those things now?" the woman said and Jaime howled in rage.

The woman moved closer to him, so that she was standing right over him and he lunged at her with both hands. She took the opportunity he provided to put another bullet in his balls. This time Jaime felt something burst and spill out onto the floor. He wanted to vomit from the pain. He wanted to kill this woman and tried to move, but the pain was so great he was assaulted by waves of darkness and nausea.

"Do you remember me?" the woman said.

"Fuck you," Jaime said, closing his eyes tight against the agony and the shifting colors.

She stepped on his groin, driving the spike of her heel into the hole where things had once been, and Jaime twitched and screamed. All thought fled his mind. There was only pain.

"Do you remember me?" she said again.

"Just let me die," Jaime said, sobbing. "Just fucking get this over with."

"Look at me," she said. "If you remember me this will all be over. Do you remember me?"

He forced his eyes open and stared at her blurring figure, waiting until she came into focus. He wanted to say he didn't know her, that she was same girl he had picked up earlier tonight. But he could tell by her expression that would only invite more pain, and he did not want that. She ground her heel in the wound and Jaime whimpered. He looked more closely at her, desperate now, casting feverishly through his memory.

She twisted her heel again. It came to him: a darkened, grungy room and a mattress stained with blood and other fluids. His eyes widened and she pulled the trigger a final time.

TWO SKULLS

The bones had been bleached dry by the sun and now were a gleaming white amidst a sea of green grass that stretched on for miles in any direction. The sun glimmered off the bones, drawing the two riders to it. They came across the rest of the body on their way to the skull—a femur here, a rib there—the body having been torn apart by whatever carrion hunters inhabited these parts. When they reached it, one of the riders dismounted, picking it up gingerly to study it, while the other kept her eyes upon the horizon in all directions.

"Be quick," the woman, whose name was Harni the Cleaved. "There is someone approaching."

"You know this cannot be rushed," Mejk the Unharnessed said, not taking his eyes from the skull.

"It may have to be," Harni said.

Hearing the urgency in her voice, Mejk looked up from the skull and cast his eyes along the horizon. "Who is it?"

"Who else," was her whispered reply.

Mejk pursed his lips and returned to the skull, turning it over carefully in his hands. All the incisors were present, but two of the molars, one on either side of the lower jaw were missing. He clicked his tongue in recognition. "It is of the tribe."

"Can you identify it?"

"We shall see," he said, letting his irritation show. Harni glanced at him, her own annoyance plain. "How long?"

"A span, no more." Harni said.

"I may not have time."

"Let the Anchored One's memory guide you."

"Yes," Mejk said.

He set the skull down upon the ground, positioning it so that the empty eye sockets cast their empty gaze upon his face. Retrieving a pouch tied to his belt, he pulled forth some of the crushed sage it held and sprinkled it upon the skull and began to recite the incantation. The words felt clumsy and unfamiliar on his tongue, though he had spoken them hundreds of times before. He was just completing the final phrases when he heard Harni's intake of breath, letting him know that whoever was approaching had arrived.

"We have claimed this ancestor. He is of our tribe," Harni said, in a clear and commanding voice, as Mejk closed his eyes and reached out to commune with what remained of this lost one's soul.

"You have no claim to the souls in this place," was the reply from one of the newcomers. He spoke in a rasping voice, as though his tongue were trying to crawl its way from his mouth.

Harni stood her ground. "These are the Untamed Lands. We have as much claim to the souls here as any tribe. This one was of our people."

"These lands have been ours since before the lost ones came," the man with the rasping voice spoke again. "We claim all that lies here."

"We dispute your claim. "

"Very well."

The jangle of the reins told Mejk that the interlopers were dismounting. A moment later Harni did the same, hissing at him as she did. Mejk did not look up from the skull. He was so near to the soul, he could feel its contours, what remained of them after so many years, and he did not want to let it loose now. If he did they might never recover it, even if they were victorious in the coming confrontation.

The soul took shape before him, shadow and dust, with hardly a form. A sign of an ancient being, one that had lived so long before it barely had any ties left with the place it had rested. Mejk urged it to reach out to him—to speak, to become—but it seemed unwilling. The slightest breeze looked as though it might dissolve the soul back to the darkness.

But finally it did become and take something like a human form before him. There was a grimacing, shadowed face and a tall lean figure. At its belt hung two skulls that grinned mirthlessly at him. Mejk was taken aback at their sight. He had never seen anything like that in all the souls he had called forth.

"Mejk," Harni's strained voice intruded into his reverie. "I need you now."

Mejk stood to go, recalling the interlopers and knowing the confrontation might have already begun. This macabre soul disturbed him and he wanted to tell Harni that they should abandon it, leave it for the people who claimed this place. He released it and prepared himself for battle.

A strange thing happened as he did so, though. The soul would not relinquish its hold on him. It pulled him back, nearer and nearer to that darkness, though Mejk fought against it. Such a thing had never happened to him before. It was impossible. The souls of the dead were there to be called forth and claimed by whoever understood the incantations. They did not do any claiming themselves.

This one did. It pulled him nearer and nearer. He cried out, even as he heard Harni cry his name again in fear and pain. What is happening? he asked himself, as he stared into the soul's eyes and saw devastation beyond all imagining, thousands lying dead.

It was only with a struggle that he pulled himself free of its gaze and tried to break loose. But as he did, he looked down at the two skulls at its belt and thought he recognized them. He peered closer and, with a growing horror, he recognized Harni on one side and himself on another. A terrible laughter echoed in his ears as the darkness claimed him.

LAST NIGHT

Another long night of keeping watch without a fire. I can smell olives on the trees. There is noise all around: the stirrings of a breeze, a restless unseen creature, or something more sinister? The air feels like a coming squall. The moon has disappeared above and I am left with only the stars till morning.

The roads are dangerous. Life is dangerous, after a time, when all the consequences from things done and choices made begin to make themselves known.

I can just make out your form through the darkness. I long to lie beside you, to press up against you and feel the contours of your body. It has been months since we had such luxury, every moment of passion has been a stolen one. A few minutes here as we rest out of sight of the road, or a few minutes there as we trade off the watch, one of us still filled with the sleep, the other driven to frenzy by boredom.

It is such an empty life now, it is hard not to feel despair, especially in these bleak moments when the darkness is my only companion. When did life become so absent of anything but survival, our days all the same, repeating themselves one after the other? I cannot recall. Every choice seemed beyond doubt, essential to our beings. Now I can hardly recall them. They seem barely to matter.

The world has just gone to fire. All of us tearing at each other in a frenzy, until nothing remains but the bones.

My bones are cold this night and I find myself shifting from foot to foot to keep warm. The air is taking on an autumnal chill. Winter will not be far behind. And what then? Where will we go? There are a hundred other questions that come to mind, but none of them bears thinking just now.

We will not be alive by then anyway, so it is pointless to worry. A sinister whisper in my head. Though I try to ignore it, I know the truth of it.

A sound, different, flowing against the current of the surrounding night, catches my attention and makes me go very still. A misplaced footstep? A sword being slipped from its scabbard? A bow being pulled taunt?

My hand is on my own sword and I crouch low, hoping I will be able to discover whoever is coming before it is too late. I wait, but no further sound comes, and slowly I allow myself to breath again. My hands are tingling from the cold and I blow on them and stuff them in my pockets as I straighten up.

Perhaps a fox moving through the forest and that is all. The thought is not reassuring. I do not believe it. There is something out there, I am certain of it. But what? Who?

I step forward uneasily, glancing over to where you lie. If someone has found us, if they are stalking toward us as I stand here, I should be waking you. But I do not. Is it doubt that stays my hand, or something else?

I decide to investigate on my own, reasoning that, so long as I do not stray too far, I can wake you with a shout or whistle if need be. This is foolish, of course. We are stronger if we stay together, easier to pick off apart. If I am fallen upon while distant from you, I may be unable to warn you.

I pick my way among the olive trees, taking care to be light on my feet, heading in the direction where I think the noise came from. Nothing stirs, the wind has gone still. The grove seems to be waiting for this drama to play itself out. The drama that is, in all likelihood, in my head alone.

I go a little way and then pause, straining at the darkness for any sign of what is out there. A sound, a scent, a shape, in amongst the shadows. There is nothing. I go a little further and stop again, resting my hand against a tree. Nothing still.

Farther and farther I go, with nothing revealed, before I begin to retreat back the way I came. There is nothing here, I tell myself, nothing at all. Still I take care as I return to you, lest my own steps betray me to the shadows.

I have a vision, as I go, of returning to the place I left you, only to find that you have gone, vanished without the trace. The night stealing you for its own. Panic seizes me and I have to resist the urge to run. You are still there, asleep, breathing steadily. I want to touch you, to take you into my arms and hold you until morning breaks. We did that once, but no more. These endless days have taken that from us as well.

It is as I am calming myself that I sense their presence and come to a halt, standing absolutely still, not even breathing. Two points of darkness, darker than the darkness, pass nearby toward where you lie. If I move now, draw my sword and fall upon them...but then I hear the approach of another from the other side of the grove. A twig snapping, and an indrawn breath, before silence descends again.

How many are there? If I attack these two now, will you awake in time to face the other? And if there are more? If I shout to wake you, will we both be able to flee and escape? So many nights we have spent making these calculations. When to run, when to attack. Only to have to do so again and again.

We called ourselves slaves once. And we were, in a manner of speaking. Our lives were nothing to those we were bonded to, and they treated us as though we were implements to be worked until broken and then replaced. We threw off those shackles and set to flames all that we had built, and in doing so left ourselves with no safe harbor to turn to. Through all the hardship, through all the battles, as our comrades splintered and factions divided, we told ourselves the suffering we endured was different. Because we were free and the choices were ours.

Noble thoughts, but untrue all the same. This misery will know no end.

I do not move from where I have stopped, listening as the three forms approach where you lie. There is a low whisper, an order, and I want to cry out, to warn you. But I do not. Instead I begin to drift away, back further into the grove. I am far enough that I almost cannot hear your cries as the swords fall.

BRIEF ENCOUNTER

"For two?" the waiter said, reaching for a stack of menus before hearing a response.

"Yes. Thanks," J said.

"This way please."

They followed the waiter as he made his way across the restaurant to a table sitting against the far wall. J and her companion sat down, smiling their thanks at the waiter, who disappeared behind them into the kitchen, moving rapidly.

"This is a big place," her companion said, looking around the room.

"Hm," J said, intent on the menu.

When she finally glanced up she saw her companion was correct. The restaurant was L-shaped and they sat near the junction of the two parts of the letter. The top part of the L, which extended from the entrance to the kitchen behind them, had more than twenty tables easily, she guessed, set in four precise rows. The other end of the L was longer and had even more tables. Maybe a third of those tables were filled now, a low murmur of conversation reaching their ears.

"What are you thinking?" her companion said, flipping through the menu. "Dim sum? And maybe some noodles?"

J did not reply. In her study of the room, she had set her eyes upon a group at a table two rows across from them. She hadn't noticed them when they first entered the restaurant—for which she was now cursing herself—and now that she had, she found herself

200

unable to stop looking. At last she forced herself to turn away—
before they noticed, and before her companion did as well.

"That sounds good," she said. "What dumplings do you want?
I'd like the pork and dill."

The conversation went back and forth ,as they debated what to
get, until the waiter came back, bringing them water and taking
down their order. All the while J agonized about the table across
the room and the people at it, specifically the one person who she
had never expected to see again. Not after their last meeting. All
she wanted to do was forget about the waiter, her companion and
their supper and watch the woman as she ate hers.

That or leave now. Leave now and find another restaurant.
Another life. It was too late for all that, though.

"Everything alright?" her companion said.

"Just distracted," J said, with a shake of her head and smile.

The time until their food arrived passed in an anguished blur. It
was all J could do not to look over again at the table, to confirm
that D was still there. To see if D had noticed her. Her companion
was saying things and J was replying, but she heard none of the
words that were spoken. Her thoughts were on that table across
the room.

Why was D here now? What was she doing in this city? Was D
here to see her? That was impossible, J knew. And yet.

The first two baskets of dim sum arrived and she took a
tentative bite of one of the dumplings, using the motion to glance
over at the table. D had her back to their side of the room, but J
felt certain—though she could not have said why—that she had
just finished turning around. J ate another dumpling, feeling ill.

"These are great," her companion said.

"Yes."

More dumpling arrived and the noodles. J tried them all, the
chopsticks trembling in her hands. She caught her companion
looking at her and attempted a smile. A flash of motion from the
corner of her eye drew her attention and she turned in time to see
D walking toward the bathroom. J was up and walking after her
before she could even think about what she was doing.

As she came to the bathroom door, she paused, her whole body
telling her to go back, to walk out of this place and never return.
She ignored it and pushed through the door. D was leaning against
the sink, facing the door, something like amusement on her face.

"You saw me." J managed to find the words, and felt immediately foolish.

"The moment you walked in. I always noticed you." D's expression did not change.

J's fingers felt numb. She realized she was clenching and unclenching her hands and forced herself to stop. "Are you here for me?"

"What? Don't flatter yourself. That was a lifetime ago." A pause. "For both of us."

"It was. I know what you're capable of, though. I know you don't forgive and you don't forget."

"There was nothing to forgive," D said. "Mostly. And I remember all of it. But like I said, that's in the past now. I'm here on other matters."

J frowned. "Why this then? Why bother?"

D laughed. "Two ships passing in the night? You know me better than that. Not my style. Can't let a moment like this just go."

"I could," J said. D did not reply. "What now?"

"Nothing. I just needed to see what you'd become."

D pronounced it as a judgment and J felt her knees tremble. She could not find the words and D did not give her the chance, brushing past her as she went out the door. J stood absolutely still for a moment, her eyes closed, until she was overcome by convulsions and had to rush for the toilet. She retched into the bowl, coughing and spitting and clutching at the cold porcelain.

How long it was until she gathered herself and rose from the floor to wash her face and return to her seat, J couldn't say. D and the rest of her group were gone from the restaurant. Her companion looked up, a question on her face. J sat down and looked away over at the empty table.

MEN OF TWILIGHT

His first mistake had been coming to this anonymous warehouse on the outskirts of the city alone and at night, without telling anyone where he was going or what he was doing. Novo was simply too caught up in the investigation. His need for justice and order, to right what he saw as wrong, had always been his greatest strength and his fatal flaw. It had led him to reveal things that those in power might wish stayed hidden. But it blinded him to many inconvenient practicalities as well. Such as, how he was going to get out of this mess of his own creation.

That was the matter at hand now, and it left him cursing his own shortsightedness. If he had texted Mary Sue before donning his full length leather jacket and heading out for the night. Or after. Or really, at any point along the continuum of events that had led him to here.

But Mary Sue, being a practical sort, would have phoned the police, who would have arrived here before he had a chance to confront this master of villainy and reveal his true plans. And that would have denied Novo his moment of triumph. A triumph that now tasted like bitter chalk at the back of his throat.

For the warehouse, empty but for the odd pieces of equipment at one end, and the flagrantly dangerous vat of acid at the center of the room, was a distraction. It was a feint by a criminal mastermind, to hide his true intentions. That was why Novo had come. He needed to know the truth. He was going to do battle with the darkness.

At best he had managed a draw, though he was the only person who would make that optimistic an assessment, given his hands and feet were bound and he was hanging from a hook suspended above the vat of acid. It did, he allowed, present some difficulties, but he had time to figure a way out of them. The hook had not started its descent into the acid, after all.

As he was pondering various scenarios for his miraculous escape, a man stepped from the shadows to where Novo had a clear view of him. His face was painted red, as were his hands, but otherwise he was dressed innocuously. He looked up at Novo and smiled. "We meet at last."

Novo felt thrilled and could hardly keep the smile from his face. At last. It was all beginning now.

"You at least owe me the courtesy of your name."

"My name is not important. But you can call me the Red Man."

Novo was silent, staring down at the man's red face and his terrible smile.

"I told you it was a terrible name." Another figure emerged from the darkness. A woman, smartly dressed, with her dark hair thrown back across her shoulders.

The Red Man looked irritated. "Not now."

"Doesn't it sound like he's playing at some racist redface thing?" the woman called up to Novo.

"The thought crossed my mind," Novo said.

"I'm not," the Red Man said. "This isn't a race thing at all. What about his name? Novo. What the hell is that?"

"I think it's cute," the woman said. "I'm Natasha, by the way."

Novo nodded.

"It sounds like a car name," the Red Man muttered.

"I'm going to make the world anew," Novo said defiantly, ignoring his perilous present circumstances.

"That's sweet," Natasha said. "See, you should think of something like that. Something that defines what you're trying to do, not just how you look. Right?"

"Why did I start this?" the Red Man said, shaking his head in annoyance. "It doesn't matter. He's in no position to make the world anew now, is he?" He chortled, a short, barking sound that made Novo wince.

"You'll never get away with this," Novo said, and immediately felt ridiculous. "Sorry, that was beneath me."

"It was beneath this entire enterprise," the Red Man agreed.

"I think it's cute," the woman said, in a voice that suggested she was practiced in giving encouragement.

"At any rate," the Red Man said, ignoring Natasha, "you are in no position to thwart my plans. You'll not be making it through this night alive."

There was a control panel at the base of the vat, controlling the hook and chains that suspended Novo, and the Red Man leaned down and pressed one of its buttons. After a pause, where it sounded as though the chains were shifting gears, the apparatus lurched into motion and Novo began to descend. It was a gradual descent, nearly in slow motion, with both the Red Man and Natasha gazing up at him idly, while he struggled against the bonds that held him. Not too much, for there was always the possibility he might somehow slip free of the hook and drop into the acid.

The Red Man grew visibly bored and began to walk from the room. "Goodbye Novo. Let's see you find your way out of this one."

"Aren't you going to reveal your plan to me?" Novo said, unable to hide the desperation in his voice. "Isn't that what this is all about?"

"I thought so, but it's been done, right?"

"He's just embarrassed. He thinks you won't be impressed," Natasha said. "Go on and tell him. I think it's very good."

"No. I'm not telling him." The Red Man flushed with anger. "Another time, perhaps," he said in parting to Novo, striding back into the shadows toward the exit.

Natasha followed behind him, stopping to give a polite wave. Novo grimaced in return.

Time was growing precariously short, he realized, looking down at the acid. He would need to find a way out of this doom and try again to determine the Red Man's nefarious plans. Novo had been certain the Red Man would tell him this night. Who didn't want to reveal their plans, after all? That was the entire point of the enterprise.

He began to kick his legs, setting the chain into motion, so that he swung in an ever-widening arc across the vat. Now, he just needed to ease the rope over the hook as the arc of his passage carried him beyond the reach of the vat. If he timed it perfectly, he would sail free of the acid and land unscathed on the ground.

He was just beginning to swing beyond its perimeter when the woman returned to the warehouse, hurrying up to the vat. She went to the control panel and turned off the mechanism, suspending him above the acid, sickeningly close, but safe. She looked up and smiled at him.

"I just couldn't bear to let him kill you like that," she said. "He so wants to tell you his plan, and he will I'm sure. He just needs the confidence. He needs you, really. He needs his nemesis."

She paused, looking around the warehouse, as though to assure herself they were alone. "Anyway. It's been a pleasure. I'm sure we'll meet again Novo. I've called the police, so they'll be here shortly to let you down. Until next time."

Natasha turned and left before Novo had a chance to process what had happened and respond. He was left to hang, alone with his thoughts. In the distance he could hear the sound of sirens.

GAMBLER'S FALLACY

The ripple of the cards upon the table, the shifting of everyone upon their chairs, the thumbing of glasses and clothes, the shuffle of money and hands: Burgess can hear it all. His eyes are closed and there is thunder in his mind, but he can hear it all. The air is redolent with the stench of rotgut whiskey, sweat and the wood burning in the stove they are all huddled near to keep out the winter cold.

Burgess opens his eyes at the sound of the door opening and sees Pederson returning within from the outhouse. A gust of frigid air makes them all tremble. Pederson takes off his coat, his breath still staining the air in clouds around his head. Everyone watches as he returns to the table and picks up the deck.

"Sorry boys," he says with a smile. "Where were we? Five card draw?"

There are grunts of assent and the cards go out. Burgess does not touch his until they are all dealt, his eyes intent upon Pederson's hands. His face feels hot in spite of the chill in the room, and his gaze goes blurry and then steady with each blink of his eyes. There is the sound of the ocean in his ears as someone stands to refill the glasses and someone else asks a question about Maggie Garneau. He thinks about saying something witty, but decides not.

The cards are dealt and he looks at them. Trip fives. He looks around the table. Everyone is looking at their cards. The bet comes to him and he throws in five dollars.

"Spending all your winter funds," Pederson says, not glancing up from his cards.

Burgess bristles. "We'll see where I stand at the end of the night."

"You'll be standing because you'll have nowhere to sit again."

Everyone laughs, even Burgess manages a chuckle, though it stings. Only this summer he ran out of funds at a game and bet a chair his mother had gifted him years before. Handcrafted, a fine piece. The thought of it makes him wince. The chairs he has now are makeshift things he built himself, as is all the furniture here in his one room shack he threw together ten years ago as a temporary home while he homesteaded this quarter. Ten years on and everything still feels temporary, especially his funds.

"At least you didn't bet your crop through," Pederson says.

He is just warming up Burgess knows, and he forces himself to stay calm. The whiskey is no help there, but he takes another gulp anyway, the liquor burning at the back of his throat.

"Of course, that's what you're doing here, isn't it? Just throwing it all away. How's the root cellar stocked? I don't recall you having much of a garden."

Several others shift uncomfortably in their seats, Pederson's words getting a little to cutting and personal. Burgess doesn't notice, he is too busy biting his tongue to stop himself from shouting at the dealer. He takes his two cards and raises the pot again without even registering what the cards are. He looks again and sees ace high. Trip fives, ace high. There is a taste of blood in his mouth.

Pederson sees his bet and raises, ten dollars, which makes Burgess quiver with doubt. They are the only two remaining in the game. The others have sat back and are watching with a mixture of fear and curiosity. They seem to guess how this will end. I will show them, Burgess thinks to himself, and he pushes the rest of his coins and bills in.

"Should be twenty or so in there, I think," he says, his voice sounding odd. He feels a surge of adrenaline. Trip fives. He is back in this game.

"Call," Pederson says without hesitation, pushing his own funds into the center of the table.

His adrenaline vanishes and Burgess feels ill, certainty of his doom taking hold. He flips over his cards to reveal the three fives.

Pederson does the same and Burgess sees three nines and the air goes from his chest.

An ugly silence that hangs over the table. Pederson breaks it, reaching out to pull his winnings close. "So, turnips for winter then."

"You goddamn cheat. You sonofabitch."

There are murmurings from others that it is only a game, that it has been aboveboard, but Burgess doesn't hear them. All he hears is Pederson's chuckle.

"It's not my fault you've got a pisspoor head for whiskey and cards."

Burgess throws his chair clattering to the floor and everyone stands, Pederson bracing himself for a fight, and the others preparing to intervene. He stalks over to his bed and pulls out the case for his revolver from beneath the bed. The gun is there, resting on the velvet molding, a few bullets scattered on the lid. He takes one and returns to the table, spinning the chamber open. Everyone, even Pederson, has their hands up, white-faced with worry.

"There's no need..." someone begins to say.

"Let me win my money back," Burgess says, slamming the gun and bullet onto the table.

"Alright," Pederson says, breathing out with his words. "What do you propose?"

"Roulette," Burgess says, pointing at the gun. "I win and I get my money back."

The others begin to argue with him, but Pederson holds up his hands and says, "I'll take that bet."

He begins to count out the money, while Burgess picks up the gun and bullet. He spins the chamber again, listening to it go. It sounds clean and moves well, which is good. His father had always told him that you could always win at Russian Roulette, provided you had a clean gun. The chamber with the bullet would be pulled by gravity to bottom of the cylinder. He cannot remember when last he cleaned it, but it was some time ago.

When the money is counted out, Burgess puts the bullet into the top chamber and slides the cylinder back into the gun. He takes a long look at everyone's faces. Their expressions blur and drip. He worries that his hand is shaking and he looks at the gun, forcing it steady. He spins the chambers, listening to them whir until they lock into place.

No one breaths as he levels the gun at his head. He forces a grin to his lips and pulls the trigger. There is the click of the chamber and then the hammer descends, all in an instant. What follows is a long and endless silence.

YOU ARE NOT WANTED HERE

The books were laughing at me. Their spines cracked and groaned as they flipped open, the pages riffling like an orchestra of wheezing accordions.

I stared at them in wonder and horror, unable to comprehend how they were moving of their own accord. Or how they managed to stay upon the shelves in spite of their convulsions. The study was filled with bookshelves, all teeming with books, and all of them now moved, animated by some malevolent spirit. Or so it seemed to me. It was not a generous, welcoming laughter that echoed from those pages. There was a menace to it, a cutting edge as sharp as their fine pages.

I backed away from the room, which I had only entered moments before, and which had seemed a quiet and somewhat austere place where I might seclude myself for some hours. Instead, I now feared for my life.

I had closed the door behind me upon entering, but now, when I tried to turn the handle, I found it locked. How that could be possible—for the mechanism appeared to allow me to lock the door from within the study, keeping intruders out—I could not say. The laughter of the books grew louder, turning into a gale force of noise. Shuddering in horror, I threw the full force of my body against the door, thinking it must be jammed and that I might be able to dislodge.

It seemed to have no effect. In fact, I was quite certain I could feel the door responding to my efforts by moving to brace itself, and perhaps even to push back against me. Panic seized me, sweat going frigid upon my forehead, as I contemplated what terrible fate might await me if the entire house turned against me.

"What do you want with me?" I cried out at the empty room.

The books did not cease their movement, but instead of laughter I heard a garbled chorus of indistinct words. "You are not wanted here."

"Then let me leave, I beg of you." I shouted, frightening myself with the tinge of madness breaking in my voice.

No words followed from the tomes, only further laughter. I fled across the room to the large window at the far end, which let in the dying embers of the day's sun. Fumbling with the latches, I tried to pry it open so that I might throw myself free of this place. The window was resistant, the latches snapping shut even as I opened them, and I pinched my fingers more than once. This led to even louder gales of laughter from the books.

"What have I ever done to you?" I said, as I searched the room for some other means of escape.

"You are not wanted here," came the reply.

"Do you take me for a fool?" I yelled in exasperation.

"You are not wanted here."

I cursed under my breath, resolving to speak no more with these recalcitrant volumes. Whatever spirit animated them sought only to taunt me, it was clear.

A stout chair sat near the window, where it would best offer a solitary reader the day's light. I judged that I would be able to lift it, and perhaps even send it through the window. Before the house had time to realize what I was about, I strode over to the chair and, grasping it by the arms, threw it against the window. It glanced off, showing no apparent ill effects, though I could hear something like a moan come from the books.

"Let me out, or I'll do it again," I said, attempting to put something like a threat in my voice.

In response, one of the books tumbled off the shelf near my head. I dodged it, letting it glance off my shoulder. Picking it up, I tore at its pages, those that I could grasp, for they continued to flutter and move as if alive. The pages above me groaned in fury, the whole house seeming to seethe and hiss at me.

"You are not wanted here."

"Damn you," I said, my anger dampening my fear, the blood

hot in my cheeks. "What right have you to turn me away? I have come here, meaning you no ill will, and this is how I am treated."

"You are not wanted here."

I picked up the chair again and threw it at the window. This time, a blemish, tiny, but there nonetheless, formed at the center of the pane. The books fluttered incoherently, as though debating what to do next. I felt flush and triumphant.

"I'll do it again. I'll break the window and escape. You cannot treat me like this. I'm a decent man. I have come here with only good intentions."

"You are not wanted here," the pages said, though they no longer sounded so resolute.

"You don't get to determine that. It is not your place. I came, bearing you no ill will. I can stay, if I so choose. In fact, I believe I shall."

With that, I seized the chair again and turned it over, sitting upon it beneath the window. The books clattered above me, some of them spilling off the shelves, even landing upon my head. But I remained resolute.

"You are not wanted here." It sounded like a desperate cry, plaintive and weak, with none of the strength that had moved the pages before.

I did not respond, remaining in the chair, my jaw set and my expression blank. The pages continued with their cries, the whole house seeming to moan and shiver, while I stayed seated. My anger cooled as the house quieted around me. I had shown my resolve and demonstrated who was its master.

Eventually, silence reigned, the pages going still above me. I could even hear the chirp of the insects in the grass outside. I rose up and wandered about my new abode, for every door was now open to me. I nodded my approval, not even hearing the faintest whispers from the study: "You are not wanted here."

OPRICHNINA AND ZEMSCHINA

I sit in the chill alone, another mile further down the road, staring up at the sky and watching my breath as it forms puffs of vanishing clouds. The air is the way only winter can make it, sharp and crisp, cutting at my lungs as it goes down my throat. Clouds are gathering, distant on the horizon, foreshadowing the storm I know is coming. Wind, snow, and tumult; the storm of our humanity will not even register.

I hope he feels as tired as I do, as hopeless and alone. Is he worn out and ready to quit, the strength to keep fighting drained by these endless hardships? No, not him. For him, the privations and difficulties are merely proof of his righteousness. The blood on his hands only demonstrates the justness of his cause and the lengths he will go to stand by it.

For me, I do not enjoy the apocalypse that he and his kind have wrought. That it is him, of all people, that I am forced to reckon with only makes it all the worse. If it were someone else, someone I did not have such a history with, it would be another matter. It would not cut so deep.

As these thoughts flit through my mind, I finger the sepulcher tome that I carry with me. It has only the dead in it now. The incantations here that my kind once worried over are now only the words of a dead tongue. He and his kind have seen to that.

He has the silver and the gold, and our lives, so many I cannot even bear to count. And now he will take this last thing too, to bring an end to this all.

There is no sense waiting further, and so I get to my weary feet and make my way to him.

He is waiting for me, sitting at a table, deep in some dark corner in a low den of impiety. It is smoke-filled and foul smelling, littered with grim-faced men who meet my eyes only fleetingly, but never cease to watch me. How many of them are his, brought to ensure that I attempt nothing? I ignore them and make my way to sit across from him.

This moment feels inescapable, the culmination of all that has happened before, and I wonder if he feels that way too.

He grins, that false smile. "It is good to see you."

"Spare me."

He nods, grimacing slightly. "You have it then?"

I take the tome out, where I have hidden it in my robes, and place it on the table in front of me. I run my fingers along the spine a final time, feeling the charge and pull of those words, longing to utter them. To curse him. To undo him.

It would do no good though. At least one of these men here is a Betrayer, I feel certain, ready to unfurl a spell on me at the first sign of sorcery on my part. To say nothing of his own abilities, of which I know only too well. It would be my death, and that is what I have come here to avoid.

I push the tome across the table and he looks down at it, not touching it. "So we are done then?"

He inhales deeply and looks up at me. "You are not so tough. You don't fool me for a moment." I do not answer and he continues, "We live in a world betrayed."

"You would know," I say, looking past him at the men scattered throughout the room. None of them has stopped looking me, but they have not moved either.

"Are you going to pretend not to understand why I have done this? Why all of us have done this? Sorcery could not continue as it was, unfettered. It would have ended with us all destroyed."

I look at him, rage burning in my cheeks. "Have you forgotten the world is real? You've reduced this to another ideology that you'll toss out tomorrow when it suits you."

"You were always a stubborn fool," he says, slumping in his chair. "We live in a world betrayed. This is what the Autarch always says. He will not rest until all sorcery is eradicated."

"All but his own."

"It is necessary."

"Do you smell that?" I say. "It never leaves your presence. The carrion will find your body when Autarch is finished with my kind."

He bites his lip and at last touches the tome, pulling his hand away as though scalded. "You have always failed to understand him. But you did trust me once. More than that. Trust me again."

"We're long past that point now," I say, standing up and turning to go.

He stands as well, his expression plaintive. I can almost believe he cares. "What will you do? Go back to scrabbling around ruins for any old washed out scraps of parchment to cling to. That is the past now, even you can see that. The future lies elsewhere, with us."

I shrug my shoulders. "I've made it here, I can make it to tomorrow. The next if I have to."

He reaches out to touch my shoulder. "You won't reconsider?"

I do not reply, turning my back on him and making my way across the room and back out into the cold. There I find three robed figures awaiting me, faces covered, fingers already moving, spells ready to be unfurled. I look from unseen face to unseen face, knowing in my soul that their faces would be ones I have seen before.

Behind me I hear the door open and turn to see him stepping out into the snow, the cowl on his robe lifted and the mask upon his face as well.

"He is madman you know," I say in a loud voice. "He will be the ruin of you all."

"We are finished here," he says, his voice gone hard. "I gave you a chance to see reason, more than you deserved. But that time is past now. I am deeply sorry."

"You just do what you have to do," I say. "Whatever you feel is necessary."

ABOUT THE AUTHOR

Clint Westgard is the author of The Shadow Men Trilogy and the science fiction epic The Sojourner Cycle, the first volume of which, The Forgotten, was published in 2015. In addition, he has published a work of historical fantasy set in colonial Peru, The Maleficio Chronicles, and a retelling of the Minotaur legend, The Trials of the Minotaur. Clint Westgard lives in Calgary, Alberta.

ALSO BY CLINT WESTGARD

Realm of Shadows
Volume One of The Shadow Men

Craitol and Renuih, two empires a world apart, divided by the desert that lies between them. A desert ruled by the Shadow Men.

An uneasy peace holds sway in both realms, hiding longstanding feuds and bitter rivalries. Until a Shadow Men raid on Renuih shatters the calm and sets in motion events no one can control.

Masiph id Ezern, unfavored son of the Imperial Vazeir, finds himself a hero following the raid. His father remains unmoved by his exploits and, in his bitterness, Masiph will find himself a reluctant participant in a plot against the empire.

As he finds himself drawn deeper and deeper into the conspiracy, he soon realizes there will be no escaping the realm of shadows, where intrigue and betrayal abound. And though the Shadow Men have gone quiet, they will not stay silent forever...

ALSO BY CLINT WESTGARD

Council of Shadows
Volume Two of The Shadow Men

Discontent continues to fester within the realms of Craitol and Renuih, fed by intrigues carried out in the shadows. As rivals and apostates struggle for supremacy, a long incubated plan begins to unfold.

Vyissan, a mysterious alkemycal practitioner arrives in Renuih, the latest strike in a long war over who shall control the secrets of alkemya and Craitol itself. He carries with him a secret that, once revealed, will reverberate across all realms. Before he can reveal it though, the conspirators against the emperor will strike their own blow.

But now, a new and more powerful menace looms on the horizon. The Shadow Men have gained the secrets of the Council Adept's alkemya and no one can be certain what they will do with it...

ALSO BY CLINT WESTGARD

Dance of Shadows
Volume Three of The Shadow Men

War with the Shadow Men looms in both realms as the consequences of the Gvers' Council in Craitol begin to make themselves known. A war that could end in glorious triumph or bitter disaster.

Doubt shadows everyone's steps, for they know there are no certainties in the desert. Especially now the Shadow Men have made the art of alkemya their own.

No one has more questions than Vyissan, for he is working in service to a cause he is no longer sure he believes in. And now he must undertake a journey with those who both loathe and fear him. Before the first sword is drawn, his life will be under threat.

But his will not be the only one, for somewhere in the desert the Shadow Men lie in wait...

ALSO BY CLINT WESTGARD

The Forgotten
Volume One of The Sojourners Cycle

Who is David Aeida? And what does he know that has so many
people pursuing him?

David doesn't know. He can't remember anything about who he is.
But he finds himself ensnared in a vicious conflict between a
religious cult and a guild that patrols the crossings between
multiple universes. They will both stop at nothing to gain whatever
knowledge he possesses. Most dangerous of all, is the implacable
hunter, known only as the Seeker, who has his own reasons for
wanting to find David.

His only hope is to recover his memories before they do. His only
ally is a woman named Meredith, and she definitely knows more
than she is telling...

Spanning both universes and the human mind, The Forgotten is an
unforgettable science fiction thriller that questions the very nature
of identity. It is the first volume of the Sojourners Cycle, an epic
that will encompass the fates of universes and humanity itself.

ALSO BY CLINT WESTGARD

The Apostate
Volume Two of The Sojourners Cycle

Laila has only one goal in mind. To have her revenge upon the
Grand Regent for all he has done to her. First, though, she needs
to find her way across the universes.

That is easier said than done. The Grand Regent's agents are still
pursuing her. As is the Society of Travellers. And the Seeker lurks
somewhere, waiting for his moment to strike.

Laila has a plan, though, and a few tricks of her own. But she will
discover that not everything is at seems. For the war she has given
her life to hides a far greater conflict.

Spanning multiple universes and the complexities of the human
mind, The Apostate, continues the incredible journey begun in The
Forgotten. The second volume of The Sojourners Cycle is an
unforgettable science fiction epic that encompasses the fates of
universes and humanity itself.

ALSO BY CLINT WESTGARD

The Maleficio Chronicles

Luisa is always more than she appears. Rumor and mystery surround her. And strange events seem to follow wherever she goes.

Born in Lima, City of Kings, to a noble family, her father so fears her true nature that he banishes her to a convent. There she falls under the suspicion of the Inquisition and decides to flee.

Disguised as a man, she embarks upon a series of wild adventures, dueling, carousing, and gambling her way across colonial Peru. But everything changes when someone recognizes her for what she truly is, and soon she finds herself fighting for her very survival.

In a world where she will always stand apart, Luisa undergoes a strange journey, marked by betrayal and murder, terrible powers and mysterious strangers. *The Maleficio Chronicles* is her incredible confession and a story like no other.

ALSO BY CLINT WESTGARD

The Trials of the Minotaur

In the fifth year of the rule of Auten the One Eyed a minotaur is
born to one of Colosi's most important families.

Taken from his mother as a newborn, exiled and cast from his
family, the minotaur vows to return to the imperial city and take his
rightful place as a patrician in the empire. But the patriarch of the
family, his grandfather, will stop at nothing to see this blemish to
his honor destroyed.

And so begins an epic journey, through lands beyond imagining,
marked by despair and exile, triumph and betrayal. At its heart lies
a quest to be free.

ALSO BY CLINT WESTGARD

The Devious Kind

A Mystery

The body of a local woman is found in a coulee on a ranch north of Loverna, her head blown off with a shotgun. New to town and the job, Constable Martin Thomas arrives on the scene as a spring snowstorm begins to wipe out all evidence before his investigation has even begun.

There is no shortage of suspects to consider. A spurned husband. A jealous lover. A betrayed business partner. And family members battling over an inheritance. All have motive and opportunity. And no one seems to be telling him everything.

As he tries to sift the truth from the lies, the snowstorm continues to build, leaving Loverna cut off from the outside world. And Thomas alone to face a killer who will do anything not to get caught.